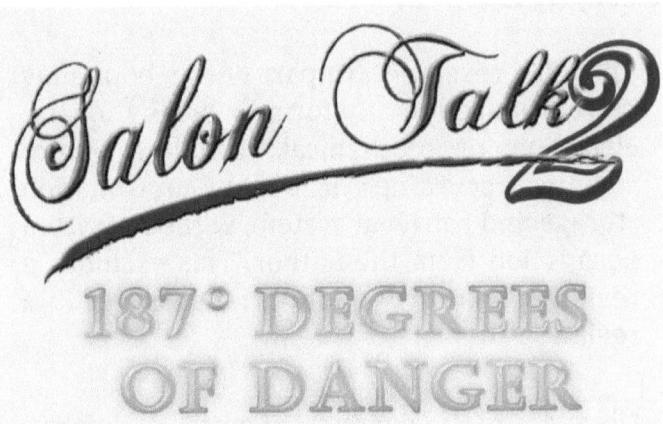

Salon Talk 2

187° DEGREES OF DANGER

Men-Tal

Library of Congress Control Number: 2011941220

ISBN: 978-0-9834307-8-0

Cover Design: Maurice Ingram and Men-Tal

Published by G Publishing, LLC

Printed in the United States of America

My Reason For Writing The Salon Talk Series

My reason for writing the Salon Talk series is to devise a captivating story that elaborates on the many beautiful and painful facets of our lives. It sheds light on happiness to drama, humor to sex to love and betrayal in relationships. Utilizing the eventful life of my main character Cognac I am able to touch on various issues that might be overbearing for some and provide a balanced perception and solution on how to address them. Essential Beauty Salon is a platform that allows me to take the spiciest and most spellbinding conversations that you love to listen to and join in on daily basis and allow you to embrace other people's perspectives on the topic that may be of some great value to you. If nothing else you will at least get a good laugh out of these conversations.

Salon Talk Q&A with Men-Tal

After the release of Salon Talk- Topic of Discussion I received a lot of much appreciated feedback. I also received quite a few interesting questions from people that I enjoyed answering. I'm sure others have similar questions and would love to know the answer to as well...so here's a few.

𝒬 What made you think that you as a man could write about the life of a woman?

A- My experience with women, and the fact that I choose not to limit myself. When I decided to title my novel Salon Talk it immediately made me think of a female main character. The title gave birth to the spicy storyline which ultimately gave birth to the main character, Cognac. It showed the balance in my writing ability. I further felt like I could pull it off because I grew up around women all of my life. I paid very close attention to their actions, and characteristics. I also listen and asked questions if it was something I didn't understand about them and I really wanted to know. The part that posed a challenge was learning about a woman's emotions and tendencies and adequately applying it to the characters in my story. I understand that these particular characteristics don't apply to every single woman, but when speaking in general they do. Besides women are human just like men, there not some strange specie from another galaxy. I feel like a writer is incapable of producing a fair, nonsexist and balanced story if he or she doesn't understand the nature and characteristics of both genders.

Q- What made you name your main character Cognac?

A- At first I named my main character Rachelle. After writing about her life the name Rachelle just wasn't spicy enough for me. It didn't have enough shock value to personify the bold lifestyle I was portraying of my main character. I needed a name that was captivating, fierce, and addictive, a name that would catch you off guard and make you think about it for a moment. A name that would make someone hate that they love it, and then I thought of Cognac. I questioned myself as far as if it were appropriate to use, and for every smidgen of a reason I could've thought of to not use it I came up with four or five great reasons why I absolutely should. And thus we have **Cognac**.

Men-Tal

Q- Why did you choose to have a female main character, and are you trying to relay a message to women?

A- I am an Author who loves a challenge when it comes to writing. Choosing a female as my main character did just that. It caused me to do research, utilize my creativity and write about the life of a woman without being sexist or bias. As far as a message is concerned it is my ambition to relay a message to both men and women. Relationships take the effort of two people to make it work so therefore I speak on the rights and wrongs of both genders. For instance I would never **JUST** teach my daughter or son that a man should never put his hands on a woman. **I teach them both that men and women should never put their hands on each other in a violent manner period**. It's foolish to believe that if you have taught your son(s) to defend themselves and fight back if someone is attacking them that they would all of a sudden abort that teaching in a domestic altercation. It is now fluently second nature and instinct. I don't want my daughter growing up feeling that it's okay for her to hit a man and believe that a man won't hit her back. NO, it is not okay, and that will be setting her up for failure. Also please know that **WORDS ARE POWERFUL!** Words are soft and sweet enough to sing a child to sleep but are also harsh and strong enough to spark wars and violence. So please be real enough with yourselves to understand that words can start domestic violence most of the time in the first place. So yes, we should be mindful and considerate about what we say. So I end my answer on this note...Men and Women should never result to violent measures and hit each other. We should adequately communicate, control our emotions and honorably talk about our problems in a peaceful manner for a positive resolution. If you are in a violent relationship get out of it. If you feel like your life would be in danger if you try to leave then never be afraid to seek help. No one is invincible so please understand that you can be helped. Love yourself, love each other, love your community, and your culture. Let it be our will to help build our community and families in a positive manner so that our children will have a brighter future before we give up.

Let's end domestic violence, and the destruction of our communities.

Q- What inspires you to follow through with your writing and getting it published?

A- My relentless thirst to be successful and my family. The depth of my struggles and failures and my will to accomplish my dreams. Realizing that if I want to be successful I can't start a project and just give up and quit, I have to follow through and thoroughly complete it. And because I am obedient to that philosophy I am currently releasing my forth book. I want to be a great writer who is well respected hundreds of years from now. So that means I have much work to do and failure or quitting is not an option.

"It is my endeavor to strive for excellence and perfection that in case I fail to do so I still achieve nothing less than greatness."
An inspirational quote by Men-Tal

<u>The Artwork</u>

Art is an incredible and major part of our lives that I feel is very underappreciated and often overlooked. Art is an expression of who we are, and how we feel. The passion, the pain, the love, and glory etc all comes from the heart and is expressed on canvas. Many people love and adore art but they probably never think about the many hours or the meticulous concentration and effort that it takes to create such beauty. The artwork in this book is all drawn by hand with a pencil, and no tracing by Men-Tal and the phenomenal Mr. Maurice Ingram, CEO of All In Mind Designs. It's well thought out concepts that help clarify the storyline as you read along. The art in this book is also available for individual purchase. We also design book covers, business cards, flyers, storyboards, portrait restoration, wedding and baby shower invitations etc. Contact information is located in the back of the book. I want everyone that purchases Salon Talk to know that they're getting a great buy and read in this novel. Thank you and please enjoy Salon Talk – 187 Degrees of Danger.

Love Broken

Passion and Flames

11:33pm New Years Eve 2010 The repetitive sound of a headboard knocked against the wall every time Cedric stroked Cynthia's juicy round ass, doggy-style. Damn, it aint nothing like some good ass make up sex. Cynthia was a moaner especially whenever he'd hit that spot. The sex faces she'd make made him want to fuck the shit out of her even harder. The flickering light from the candles highlighted the beautiful definition of her frame. She loved the way he pulled her hair, and every time he smacked her on the ass it would send erotic impulses to her pussy making her juices produce ridiculously.

"YES DADDY, GIVE IT TO ME HARDER BABY, FASTER! I love it when you give it to me Doggy-style, gaud damn!" Cynthia said intensely as she looked back at him.

Cedric got a good grip on her shoulder length hair with one hand and pulled as he continuously laid the wood to her like a reckless lumberjack. Cynthia was a freak who got off on ruff sex, and loved it when he called her names and choked her sometimes.

"I love it when you pull my fucking hair, Damn you're about to make me fucking cum!" Cynthia said loud as fuck as she clutched the bed sheets, stiffening her body, climaxing something serious.

Cedric could feel her wetness all around his balls, trickling down his inner thighs. His pulse and breathing accelerated the more his cum built up ready to explode. The feeling grew more and more intense by the second as he tried to get in as many strokes as he could. He stroked her more and more till he could no longer hold back then pulled it out and jacked his cum all over her pretty round ass. Cynthia turned around and grabbed his dick, squeezing out the rest of his nut. She twirled her tongue around the head and then sucked it slow and passionately. She knew she completed her mission as Cedric's body began quivering while cuming extremely in her mouth. Cynthia swallowed every last drop till he could no longer take no more and pulled it out of her mouth.

"I takes care of mines, don't forget that shit." She said as she got up and walked into the bathroom to take a shower.

"I feel you, sweet thang, that shit was the bomb." Cedric replied with his heavy breathing decreasing back to normal.

He lied back on the bed, placing his hands behind his head thinking to himself how much he loved her. He couldn't wait to surprise her tonight by proposing to her at the Chocolate and Cream Theme New Years Eve Ball to bring in 2011. He started getting sleepy and his eyelids were barely staying open. Just as he started drifting off he was alarmed as Cynthia's cell phone started vibrating. He was shocked that she had forgotten to take it with her into the bathroom like she normally does. He reached over, grabbed it and looked at the screen. He was even more shocked that she had forgotten to put her security lock on it. She had been acting very secretive with her phone lately and this was the perfect opportunity to see what was going on. Part of him felt like he was violating her privacy by going through her phone, but he felt like their relationship should be open with no secrets. He couldn't look through it fast enough as he did his best to see all that he could see before she got out the shower and came back into the room. DAMN...he found the evidence he was looking for when he saw that it read she had a video message from Damon. Fire immediately shot through his fucking veins as he thought to himself who the fuck is this nigga! He clicked on the video and watched carefully. He didn't want to believe his eyes at first and stared at the screen with his mouth slightly opened in disbelief. His heart pounded through his chest and his jaws tightened. Veins surfaced at the sides of his temples as the whites of his eyes took a slight reddish tent. Enraged is just an understatement of the way he felt when he saw the video of Cynthia sucking the fuck out of Damon's dick. Damon was palming her head and stroking her mouth like they were making a porn video for Head Giving Nurses Vol 6. Cedric felt like he had the wind knocked out of his chest with a sledge hammer, leaving him feeling empty inside. A text message appeared right after the video message which read "Hello baby. How's my sweetheart doing? I want to explore that sexy ass body of yours again. When you gone cut that muthafucka Cedric loose and come fuck with a real nigga? Fuck that nigga." Cedric became so furiously heated that his ears began to burn. He walked over to the dresser, and grabbed the bottle of Moet that they were pouring from. He turned the bottle up and took a big gulp of it from the neck as it sloppily spilled down the side of his jaws. He headed towards the bathroom to bust the door open, and smack the shit out of her. He stopped himself and tried to think more rational. If he beat her ass, he'll be the one locked up, and she and Damon will still be out here fucking anyway. However, somebody had to pay and rationality was becoming obsolete by the second! He had been honest to her, and never cheated on her. By him investing a lot of time, love, energy, and money into this relationship her infidelity left him feeling straight up violated, and betrayed. He walked over to the closet and grabbed a square brown designer case from off of the top shelf. He sat it down on the dresser then opened it up, reached inside and pulled out a Nine-millimeter pistol that he kept over her house for protection. He uttered to himself "This nigga knows my name?! This nigga fucking my babe?! Ima kill this muthafucka!" Cedric heard Cynthia turn the water off in the shower and step out. He hurried and laid the phone faced down on the nightstand. He placed the brown case the pistol was in on the side of the dresser down on the floor. He quickly turned off the nightlight and quietly leaped back in the bed. He carefully put the pistol on the floor just on left side of the bed where he was laying. He quickly lied back and pretended to be sleep. Cynthia dried off and swiftly tip-toed through the cold hallway, back into the room. She tossed the towel on the dresser and crawled in the bed and laid her head on Cedric's chest. She gave him a wet kiss on the neck and uttered sensually "MMmmmmmmmmmm I can go for a little bit more of this dick."

She started lightly sucking on his chest nipple as she slid her hand down his abdomens. She grabbed his dick and slowly stroked it but he never responded. She figured maybe he was in a deep sleep so she gave him a goodnight kiss on the cheek. She lied back on the bed and closed her eyes. Cedric calmly laid there calculating what he was about to do.

"How did your meeting go last Friday?" Cedric asked out the blue.

Cynthia paused for a second, and then responded.

"It, it went okay... Why you ask?" Cynthia asked slightly caught off guard, but tried to keep her composer.

"Oh I was just asking." Cedric answered calmly as he remained lying on the bed with his eyes closed.

Cynthia realized that she had fucked up and forgot to take her cell phone with her when she went to take a shower. She quickly glanced to her right and saw that her phone was lying face down on the nightstand. She reached over and picked it up to see the time and laid it back down. She took a slow deep breath then laid her head on her pillow and closed her eyes. After about fifteen minutes of pondering on her unfaithful lifestyle she fell asleep. She dreamt of her and Damon having some wild heated sex. They were on the balcony of some high rise loft located Downtown Detroit just off of the river. It was a beautiful full moon that night and the breeze felt fantastic whisking up against their skin. Damon's hands gripped her waist as she was bent over doggy-style holding on to the black iron railing. High rise sex while staring down over the beautiful city lights is mind blowing. Her hands clinched the bar tightly and her breathing accelerated. She made the nastiest sex faces as she was getting the shit fucked out of her. She did her best to hold back her screams and not disturb the neighbors. From out of nowhere she heard Cedric's voice as he stepped onto the balcony!!!

"Oh that's how the fuck it's laying?!!!" Cedric asked as he pointed his pistol at them.

"Cedric!" Cynthia yelled in shock as she and Damon immediately tried gathering themselves. They eased backwards as far as they could till they backed up against the railing. They looked through the thick bars of the railing, down on the ground and saw nothing but a painful drop awaiting them.

"Hold on man, please I can explain, Big Dog!" Damon nervously pleaded.

"Explain this muthafucka!" Cedric said as he pulled the trigger and opened fire at them.

Cynthia gasped for air as she abruptly woke up out of her nightmare with her chest palpitating. Her heart felt like it was an unborn child rapidly kicking through her chest. She looked over at Cedric and saw him laid out sleep next to her. She slowly calmed herself and lied back down. She closed her eyes and tried going back to sleep. She regretted ever meeting Damon as guilt filled her heart. She thought about the videos that were in her phone, and how she desperately needed to erase them. She thought about the text messages that she had just sent Damon asking him to stop texting and calling her right before she and Cedric fucked. She then thought how she had laid her phone faced up on the nightstand. All of a sudden reality hit her like a Mike Tyson punch to the brain! Last time she used her phone it was faced up, and when she just checked the time, it was faced down so she knew Cedric had looked into her phone. Her eyes immediately opened wide and to her surprise she saw Cedric standing over her. She looked at his hand and noticed he was holding a pistol.

"Cedric, what are you doing?!" Cynthia asked as she slid her way out the other side of the bed.

"Don't move another muthafucking inch! Stand your ass still." Cedric said firmly as he stood there ominously.

"Cedric baby talk to me, please put the gun down baby please?!" Cynthia pleaded with tears in her eyes.

"So you been out cheating on me huh, Cynthia?!"

"No baby I swear, I would never cheat on you, baby. What are you talking about?!" Cynthia asked very nervously.

"So you just gone fucking lie to me like that? For real?" Cedric asked.

Cynthia wished she could just wake up out of a dream, and this moment would've been only a nightmare...but it wasn't. She didn't know if the truth was going to kill her first or if Cedric was. All she knew was that she was dying inside from not knowing what was about to happen next. She never saw this side of Cedric before.

"Baby please, I can explain!" Cynthia whined.

"Oh now all of a sudden you can explain now huh, Cynthia? Explain to me how you fucked this nigga Damon, and sucked this nigga dick and videoed the shit! Explain to me that shit! Everything that I've fucking invested in this relationship, my love, my time, my fuckin hard earned money, and you gone play me like this?!!" Cedric yelled as spit flew out of his mouth and sporadically drizzled on Cynthia with every word he spoke.

"Where are you getting this from?!" Cynthia asked as her heart raced a million miles a second.

"You gone keep playing me like I'm stupid?! Get the fuck up off the floor and getcha phone!" Cedric yelled.

Cynthia got up slow and nervously while resentfully easing her way to the phone.

"Hurry up and grab the damn phone!" Cedric reiterated as he picked up the phone off the nightstand and tossed it at her.

With her hand shaking nervously, Cynthia finally picked up the phone off of the floor.

"Now open it and look at the last video that was sent to you!"

Cynthia's body felt hollow and lifeless as she stared at the phone in disbelief. She couldn't believe Damon would send a video to her phone, especially after she told him from jump she was in a relationship. On top of that she had just asked him to stop sending her messages and calling her.

"Play the fucking video, Cynthia!" Cedric yelled.

Her hand continued to tremble as she pushed play and stared at the video. Tears instantly streamed down her face as she listened to the once pleasing sounds of sex translate to momentary frequencies of trauma. Cedric made her check her last text message as well. She closed her eyes in disbelief and sighed

"I can't believe this." Cynthia uttered.

"You can't believe what? You can't believe that I caught yo stupid ass cheating, or you can't believe you did that bullshit? Lying to me the whole fucking time, talking about you was at your mother's house! And on top of that, you said that you were at a meeting, I guess you forgot that you told me that you were at your mom's watching some kids. I can't believe this shit." Cedric said as he slightly paced the floor back and forth unable to keep still.

"I'm sorry baby, I promise I'll never do it again baby, I swear." Cynthia pleaded, as her heart pounded.

Cynthia sat the phone down on the bed and carefully eased her way over to Cedric, and then gently put her hand onto the barrel of the gun slowly pointing it in the other direction. She got chest to chest with Cedric then looked up at him, but he didn't want to look into her eyes so he turned his head. He still loved her incredibly but hated her for what she did. She placed her head on his chest and listened to the sound of his heartbeat.

"Baby please put the gun down, that thing can kill me, boo. I'll do anything you tell me to do baby I swear. I made a bad decision, I'm so sorry Cedric, I love you." Cynthia uttered sincerely with a watery face.

"I'm not gone fucking kill you, I love you. I'm the one that fucking loves you, not him. I can't believe you did me this way." Cedric said as tears slowly rolled down his face and a lost stare out of the window.

"I'm sorry baby." Cynthia said as she hugged him while trying to calmly ease the gun down onto the night stand.

They both cried for a couple of seconds and then her cell phone chimed again.

"It's that nigga, aint it?! I know it is!" Cedric said as every muscle in his body tightened.

"Forget him, baby. Just give me the gun." Cynthia pleaded as she pulled on the gun to take it away.

"Stop, let it go, Cynthia. I got it." Cedric stressed.

"Please, Cedric give me the gun!" Cynthia said as she yanked on the gun.

"Stop before you make the gu...!" Cedric silenced, petrified by what he didn't want to see happen.

The gun went off, and Cynthia just looked at him for a couple of seconds............then fell to the floor. Cedric was momentarily petrified!

"Oh my God baby!... Why would you yank on the fuckin gun?!" Cedric asked. He dropped to his knees, frantically snatching the sheets off of the bed, placing it over the wound. He did his best not to panic as he applied pressure, trying to stop the perfuse bleeding from her stomach. "Oh God, please help me. Help me God, please."

Cynthia's body quivered as she barely managed to utter with blood accumulating in her mouth "Cedric, don't let me die."

Cedric pleaded desperately. He talked to her to calm her, thinking if he can keep her relaxed it would help slow the bleeding.

"Just relax baby, just relax. Everything is gonna be alright, just hang in there baby please."

Cynthia's eyes looked glazed over as she lied there lifeless. Cedric frantically looked around for her cell phone. He got up and grabbed it off of the bed and rushed back over to her. Nervously fumbling his fingers across the buttons he dialed 911.

"911, may I help?" The operator asked.

"Hello, I need a medic! My girlfriend has been shot. I'm located at..." Cedric said then abruptly paused what he was saying as he looked at Cynthia.

He knew that she was dead and just hung up the phone while the operator kept saying hello trying to find out what was going on. He went into a delusional daze as he sat there on the floor helpless in disbelief. After about a minute of crying he carefully laid Cynthia's body on the floor then picked up his pistol and placed the barrel up under his chin. With tightly closed eyes, and breathing heavily his hand trembled as his finger gradually inched on the trigger.

"If it wasn't for that nigga in our mix this shit would've never happened, my future wife would still be here." Cedric said while gnashing his teeth and tears streaming down his face.

He thought to himself why did this have to happen to him...he was a good man... If he turned his self in he'll surly do life in prison. Wicked thoughts sparked in his mind like a flame from a lighter. Its Damon's fault and he should be the one who has to pay for this tragedy. He shouldn't be able to just get off Scott free when he knew all along Cynthia had a man...he should pay...dearly.   Cedric took the gun away from his chin, sat it on the floor, and then picked up her cell phone and text Damon. "Hey baby, Cedric is dead to the world sleep, and I wanna see you." Then Damon replied "When, tonight?" Cedric texted back "Yes, tonight." Damon text her back "Come on baby, I'm waiting." Cedric texted Damon back "Text me your address because I don't quite remember it, and I'm on my way shortly, bay." Damon texted back "18764 Witten St. I'm sleepy as hell so I might be knocked out when you get here, but the door will be unlocked. See ya when you get here, sexy" Damon text back.

1:38 am New Years Cedric arrived at Witten Street and made a right turn. He peered through the thick flurries of snow flakes, looking for the address as he carefully cruised up the block. He located the house, and looked around observing the scene. He drove to the corner and turned left and parked close by the alley. The sound of New Years gun fire had slowed up but you could still hear a little of it here and there. Cedric was to angry to give a fuck about being scared of getting hit by a stray bullet as he patiently sat in his car for about twenty more minutes. He eventually got out of the car, tucked the gun in his waistline and concealed it with his shirt. The street was silent; you could hear the snow crackling under his feet as he proceeded up the street. As he approached Damon's house he carefully looked around at the neighbor's homes to see if anyone was looking. He quietly walked up on Damon's porch and slowly turned the knob opening the screen door, and did the same with the main door. He quietly shut the door behind him and carefully looked around as he entered the dimly lit living room. He drew his gun, took the safety off and slowly pulled back the slide, releasing one of the bullets from the clip into the chamber. He peeked into the dining room and then silently made his way through the kitchen. He looked in the den and saw that the downstairs was clear; Damon had to be upstairs. He eased his way to the living room and peeked around the corner and looked up the staircase. Quietly he crept his way up the stairwell, stepping up the left edge of the stairs along the side of the wall to avoid making the stairs squeak. He made it to the second floor without a sound, and his gun elevated just above his shoulder. He peeped into the room to the right which was open and saw that no one was in there, so he figured that he was in the room across from it. He opened the door quietly and eased in the dark room where Damon was sleeping vulnerably. He quietly pushed the door up till it was partially closed behind him. The room was barely illuminated by moonlight and the glare of a streetlight. Cedric quietly stood there in the darkness. Damon sort of woke up and partially looked around and saw nothing out of the ordinary. Damon wondered what happened to Cynthia and if she was still coming. He knew that she may have been with Cedric and couldn't get away but when you're drunk and want some pussy you don't really give a fuck about what nobody else thinks. Damon grabbed his cell phone then laid his head back down on the pillow, and text her. Cedric had Cynthia's phone in his jacket pocket as it lightly vibrated twice. Damon was slightly thrown off when he heard a phone vibrate. He didn't see anyone but sort of figured maybe it was Cynthia trying to scare him.

Men-Tal

"Girl, come get yo sexy ass in this bed and ride this dick... I know you over there because I just heard your phone go off." Damon said as he laid there holding his dick.

Cedric came forth partially into the light, and pointed his gun at Damon. Damon was shocked as his heart raced a million miles a second. He leaped up out the other side of the bed, and fell back up against the wall, nervously holding his hands up.

"What the fuck, dude?! Hold on, man! Who the fuck are you?" Damon asked, breathing heavily and fearing for his life.

"Nigga, you know exactly who the fuck I am." Cedric answered.

"Dog, I don't know you, man. You got the wrong guy, bro." Damon pleaded.

"No, Mr. Damon...I have the right guy, trust me." Cedric said as he shot Damon in the leg making him fall to the ground.

"Please man, don't kill me! I'll give you anything I got man, just don't kill me! Please dog." Damon yelled and pleaded with his hands shaking like a muthafucka.

"Don't kill you?! Nigga, did you think of this when you fucked my wife?!" Cedric replied.

"Your wife?! Who, who is your wife?" Damon asked.

"You gone play stupid, Damon? Seriously? All Ima say is... Cynthia. The videos, the text messages saying fuck me. Need I say more?" Cedric asked as he tossed her phone at him.

Damon dropped his head and knew that there wasn't too much more he could say to the man whose wife he was fucking. He figured he was about to die so he might as well try to quickly grab his gun from the night stand drawer. He made an attempt to lunge for the drawer but Cedric shot him in the side, stopping him in his tracks. Barely breathing, Damon slowly uttered with blood seeping from his mouth "Man...I didn't know she was your wife, dude."

"IT DON'T FUCKIN MATTER IF SHE WAS MY WIFE, MY WOMAN, OR MY BITCH! Muthafucka you knew she was with somebody and you knew that you were violating him!" Cedric stressed.

"I didn't know man!" Damon screamed as Cedric shot him in the other leg.

"It aint like you gave a fuck either! You sound like you wouldn't have done it if you knew it was me she was with! That's

Men-Tal

bullshit!" Cedric said as he shot him in the arm.

"HELP ME PLEASE! SOMEBODY HELP ME!" Damon yelled as he tried to slide across the bloody floor with one hand.

"Shhhhhhhhhh hush Damon before you wake the neighbors, no one's coming to rescue you. You're better off praying and asking for forgiveness before you die... But then again me being me, and pissed because you fucked my girl...I'll just kill you before you say Amen."

Damon started crying, hoping that Cedric would let him live.

"Hush, hush, hush don't cry...everyone knows that it aint right to fuck with another man's woman or wife or whatever. You shouldn't have fucked her, Damon... I mean really...if you think about it, it's part of your fault that she's dead now,   but since you wanted to be with her..." Cedric said as he stopped what he was saying and just looked at him.

"Dead?" Damon asked as his face straightened in disbelief.

"Yes, Damon she's dead, and it's all because of you. And now you got to pay. Because aint no fuckin way you gonna be out here living it up and I'm serving life behind bars for some wrongful shit y'all did. **Fuck that**." Cedric stated.

"Please man, I'm sorry." Damon said pitifully.

"Sorry?...Sorry? SORRY DIDDN'T DO IT DAMON, YOU DID! BUT SINCE YOU WANTED TO BE WITH HER...I suppose you can, and it is my honor...to grant your wish." Cedric said.

"PLEASE MAN DON'T, PLEASE MY BROTHA!" were the last words that spilled out of Damon's mouth before catching a bullet in between the eyes.

Cedric walked over to Damon and stood over him ominously.

"Well...you wanted to be with her muthafucka, now be with her...on the other side, nigga." Cedric fired one more round in Damon's head.

Momentary insanity had become him as he just turned and walked away. With a lost stare and a pistol in hand he walked down the stairs and out the front door leaving it wide open. A neighbor who was alarmed by the muffled screams and gun fire was looking out her upstairs bedroom window and saw Cedric walking away from Damon's house with his gun in hand.

Men-Tal

Later that day around noon, Cedric was sitting on the hardwood floor in the dining room of his home with a lit blunt in his hand as he was talking on the phone to Regina. A loaded pistol lied next to a glass of vodka on the floor by his side as he explained how his life took an unexpected, unfortunate twist of fate. Regina was devastated by what she was hearing. She needed to slow the conversation down for a second so she could gather her thoughts.

"Just calm down, take a deep breath, we have to think, and pull all of this together." Regina said over the other end of the phone.

"Aint no way out of this, Regina. Aint no way out!!... I can't believe this shit! I aint even the one who brought this bullshit into our relationship...it's not right." Cedric said as he was slowly falling apart.

"Cedric, calm down I need you to focus right now. It has to be a way out of this." Regina requested.

"Fuck calming down! I hate that I ever met that bitch! Her fucked up ass emotions and actions wrecked **MY LIFE**. She never wanted to talk about our problems she would always walk away or brush it off. All she had to do was be rational and level headed, and now……." Cedric said as he abruptly stopped talking, thinking that he heard a noise.

"…Cedric…Cedric, Cedric you there? CEDRIC…Cedric, I need you to talk to me. What's wrong, what's going on?" Regina asked nervously after a couple of seconds of silence.

"……….Hold on….." Cedric uttered as he sat the phone down.

He noticed multiple black figures moving from the side of his house towards the front and getting into position. He knew in his heart that it was the police, and they were about to break through the door at any second. So he picked up his glass of vodka, and took a huge gulp. Then he looked at his blunt for a second then put it to his lips, and took a strong toke and inhaled the toxins. He sat the glass of vodka back down on the floor then picked up the pistol, cocked it, and placed the barrel up under his chin.

"Cedric, what's going on?" Regina asked frantically.

Cedric could still hear Regina's voice screaming through the phone while it was on the floor, but chose to ignore her. He had made up his mind.

Men-Tal

"You bitches will never take me alive or lock me up." Cedric uttered as he exhaled a stream of marijuana smoke into the air.

"Cedric...CEDRIC...CEDRIC!!!!!!!! What's going on?!" Regina yelled.

A single shot of gunfire went off simultaneously as the Detroit Police Department broke through the front and side doors. They braced themselves as they cautiously moved forward through the home with their guns drawn. Just to discover a suicide victim slumped over on the floor bleeding next to a spilled glass of vodka, and a blunt that was still burning.

MZ "CAN'T TELL HER SHIT!" COGNAC

Eight Months Later... Essential Beauty Salon.

"Coney, I need you listen to me, please." Regina stressed trying to get Cognac to sincerely pay attention to her.

"I'm listening, go ahead." Cognac replied slightly frustrated, not wanting to be lectured right then.

"Look, when it comes down to relationships the most valuable thing that's at stake is the heart. And just because you aint putting your heart on the line doesn't mean that another person aint. That's why you have to be extra careful when you dealing with folks out here. Yeah   in the beginning it may just be a physical thing, sex with no questions asked, but when you're dealing with something beautiful and divine as sex, it's guaranteed that feelings and emotions will eventually become a factor. And trust me not all the time will the outcome be pleasant, just think of the men and women that lay six feet deep in a grave." Regina said as she dropped the truth on her younger cousin, Cognac.

"Damn Regina! Why you always gotta get deep on a sista? Just because those things happened to somebody else don't mean it's going to happen to me." Cognac said.

"It aint that I'm trying to get all deep on you like that, but sometimes you might not be thinking deep enough about things out here." Regina answered.

"I mean it's like you criticize everything." Cognac said as she showed a slight bit of frustration.

"Is it criticism or is it me trying to give my cousin some sound and positive advice?" Regina asked.

"Its sound advice, but you don't have to brake things down to me like I'm a blind little girl that aint never dated a guy before." Cognac expressed.

"Do you understand that if something happens to you, and I never even tried to say anything to you about it that I could never forgive myself? Just look at what happened to Cynthia and Cedric. Cedric killed Damon and shot himself, and Cynthia is in a coma with a great chance she could die. And if she does ever make it out of this coma she is going to have to live with the haunting fact that if she would've never been messing around cheating on her man neither one of these men would be dead right now. That guilt will definitely ride her to her grave. I love you Coney, and you know I'm in your corner" Regina said looking Cognac in her eyes.

Cognac took a deep breath and looked away.

"I love you to, but you aint gotta watch over me. I know you my big cousin, but I'm grown now." Cognac said as she looked back at Regina.

"Coney, you dealing with two drug dealers who don't even like each other. They're both probably heavily involved in the streets, and what's worse is that after you've been recognized as one of these dudes girlfriend your life is endangered daily, and you got a son to live for." Regina stressed.

"Regina I know you love me, but like I said I'm grown and I know how to take care of myself and my son, big cuz. Stop worrying so much." Cognac said as she sipped her ever fresh Papaya juice.

"I mean, why do you even like these type of dudes? Why you don't you just get with a good brotha who will treat you right?" Regina asked.

Cognac scoffed at what Regina said and replied "Aint no good men out here last time I checked."

"The only reason why you feel this way is because you choose to date those nobody, low-life brotha's. All brotha's are not bad; you just have to be selective about who you're dating." Regina replied sincerely.

"Like I said before I'm grown, life is a gamble and I definitely got this on lock, end of discussion." Cognac said as she turned to walk away.

Regina grabbed her by her arm and gained her attention once more.

"We family...So don't walk off be bitter with me because I have you in my best interest." Regina impressed.

"Look--" Cognac said before abruptly being cut off.

"No, you look! Ima say this one last thing then Ima leave it alone... Life...is definitely a gamble...and every day we take a chance on something, but just remember... The greater the risk the more detrimental the outcome can be. You can crap out...but you can't live twice. End of discussion." Regina said as she walked back up front into the salon. Business was full throttle; women were getting their hair-doo's whipped, nail manicures, and having spicy conversation about men and everything else.

Regina had a client who had just walked in right before her hair appointment was about to be cancelled.

"Wsup Regina?" Regina's client, Tanisha asked as she sat down in the hydraulic chair.

"Giiirrrll you are the master at barely making it before you lose your appointment time." Regina said.

"You know I have to make a grand entrance when I step into the building" Tanisha said as she took the scarf off of her head.

"Dayumn! It looks like chickens been fighting in yo head!" Regina said with wide eyes.

"It aint that bad, quit playing." Tanisha said.

"Playing? Girl Bye!" Regina said as she picked up her pocket calculator off of the counter and started pressing a whole bunch of numbers as she starred at Tanisha's head.

"What are you doing?" Tanisha asked.

"Adding up what its gone cost you." Regina said.

"It's going to be the same price as always aint it?" Tanisha asked as she looked at Regina with her eyebrows raised.

"Nall because this time I have to tally up the other fee's." Regina added being funny.

"What other fees?" Tanisha asked.

"The demolition and reconstruction fees! Not to mention ya late grand entrance fees." Regina said being sarcastic.

Benita who was across from them on the other side of the counter washing a ladies hair had to add her two cent.

"Yeah and speaking of grand entrances you made a grand entrance alright, a grand entrance into the wrong building. You don't need a hair stylist, you need a magician!" Benita said being funny.

"Whatever girl, don't you start." Tanisha replied as she leaned back and let Regina start on her hair.

"Don't worry Tanisha, if she charges you an arm and a leg you can always come to me because De' Juan takes care of his people boo." De' Juan said jokingly while he curled Clarrisa's hair.

"Don't be trying to steal my customers Mr. Slick" Regina said with a smile and a raised eyebrow.

"You better be quiet and leave De'Juan alone before he steal your man. You see he got them diva ass arched eyebrows." Clarisa said cracking a joke on De' Juan.

"Well at least I got eyebrows to arch and I aint walking around with no eyebrows looking excited at all times!" De' Juan responded causing a rumble of snickering in the room.

"Oh yeah? Well maybe I'll look over excited if I found out that you actually dated women and wasn't taking it up the tail pipe" Clarisa responded a little harder.

"Oh you aint gotta worry about who I'm dating trust me, I love women just like you love eating big boxes of glazed donuts, A WHOLE DAMN LOT!" De' Juan said with his arched eyebrow raised.

"Boy Bye! The only thing you love about women is being able to talk about sexy men and shopping." Clarissa said with an incredulous look on her face.

Clarissa looked over at Antonio who was getting ready to manicure a ladies feet.

"And if I was Antonio I'd watch my drinks because Little Richard over here might slip him an E-pill just to get close to him if you know what I mean." Clarissa added.

"Hey please don't put me in yall mess." Antonio said while laughing and setting up to do Michelle's toes.

"What you need to do instead of being all up in my business is start drinking fat free water so you can stop looking like a busted can of biscuits everyday. I thought you was the Michelin Man walking up in here today." De' Juan said with an attitude as things started getting heated.

"Come on yall chill out with all that. We are supposed to be professionals trying to build the reputation of Essential Beauty Salon and take it to the next level." Antonio added.

"Don't be trying to act all grown up and like you don't be cracking up at people's jokes, Negro." Peaches said sarcastically picking on Antonio while doing her clients hair.

"I'm as professional and grown as it gets, sweet thang." Antonio replied.

"You shole is grown baby, grown all over." Said Michelle looking directly into Antonio's eyes as she sexually nibbled the side of her index finger and placed her feet inside of the foot spa.

"I see you a sweet talker today, huh." Antonio said.

"I'm just calling it like I see it, sexy man." Michelle replied.

"Well in that case thank you, sweetie." Antonio said as he grabbed a towel off of the counter.

"No...it's thank you for making my nails look so good all the time." Michelle added.

"No problem. Hey look I'll be right back, I gotta go get something out of my locker so you just sit here and soak them pretty little feet of yours." Antonio said as he stood up and walked to the back room.

"Yes daddy." Michelle said flirtatiously.

Antonio went into the back room and shut the door behind him. He notice Peaches on her tip toes trying to reach the paper towel up in the cabinet.

"Damn Peaches your ass look so damn delicious." Antonio uttered under his breath to himself as he lustfully glanced over at her 32, 22, 40 inch voluptuous figure, and decided to walk over and assist her.

"Can I get that for you?" Antonio asked as he reached over her shoulder from behind grabbing the paper towel for her.

"Boy you scared me!!" Peaches said as she turned around with an accelerated heartbeat.

"You know I aint gone let nothing happen to you sweetie." He said as he looked her in her eyes, and handed her the paper towel.

"Boy don't be trying to run that game on me like you be running on them lil hoes out there." Peaches said as she looked up at Antonio.

"Now why you gotta go there? Aint nobody trying to run no game on you." Antonio replied.

"Antonio, you say the same stuff to me that you say to them females out there. So what makes me special?" Peaches said as she sat the paper towel down on the counter while focusing on his every word.

"Peaches, you aint heard me say nothing sexual or provocative to them. What are you talking about?" Antonio softly grabs her hand.

"You already know what I'm talking about. Hey sweetie, okay sweetie, the same stuff you say when you call me sweetie."

Peaches answered as she eased her hand away from his.

"No it's not, it's just a figure of speech when I'm talking to them. I mean it totally different when I'm talking to you." Antonio said in a frustrated manner.

"What are you getting all mad for?" She asked.

"I aint mad but I hate dealing with them unnecessary emotions. You always conjuring up something that aint true and you run with it as if you're right." Antonio said as he looked away and back at Peaches.

"First of all stop looking at a woman's emotions as something unnecessary. Try understanding that a woman gets fed up with all the B.S and fairytales these dudes run on them every single day. Yall guys always want a woman that can't nobody else touch or have but yall still want to be a hoe and screw every female in the city." Peaches replied eloquently.

"Oh I see what your problem is. You've been hurt and now you want to make every dude you meet pay for another dudes mistakes."

"Antonio, what is it that you want from me because we arguing like we a couple?" Peaches placed her hand on her hip.

"Maybe I want you to give me a fair chance. Maybe I want you to stop playing these unnecessary back and forth games. One minute you act like we together; we date, we cook for each other, we have sex, and then you turn right around and you tell me that we're just friends and you aint ready to be in a relationship. I just want you to be straight up with me and stop playing these little scary mind games."

"Maybe I would like to if your flirtatious actions with other women didn't scare me." Peaches said as she looked him dead in his eyes.

"Look ...I know we got clients out there so can we finish this conversation up over dinner after work please?" Antonio pleaded.

"Maybe." Peaches replied as she walked back up front.

Antonio just shook his head and looked at her as she walked back up front and shut the door behind her.   In the mean time while Michelle was waiting on Antonio she was gossiping with her girl Kelly who was sitting next to her waiting to get a pedicure as well.

"I like those sandals Cognac got on." Kelly said.

"They alright, but I got some that's way better than those." Michelle replied.

"She must have gotten them from that new dude she been kicking it with." Kelly looked over at Michelle then back at Cognac's sandals.

"What new dude?" Michelle asked with a subtle look of resentment on her face.

"Some dude. Look like he a baller. I seen him a couple of times when he'd come up here and Cognac would go outside and get in the car with him." Kelly answered.

"Baller? I doubt it." Michelle said with a stank look on her face.

Michelle looked over at Cognac with thoughts full of envy. She couldn't hide the little stank bitch personality side of herself and decided to dip into Cognac business and try to put her on blast.

"Wsup Miss, Cognac? I heard you was big pimpin now days." Michelle said as she looked over at Cognac.

"I aint pimpin I'm just doing me. I aint doing nothing nobody else can't do." Cognac replied real brief.

"When you gone teach a sista how to work that magic?" Michelle asked.

"Michelle, you got the same thang I got, and I can't teach you how to work that, you on your own." Cognac answered as she continued wiping down her desk where she keeps her hair supplies she uses on her clients.

Michelle leaned over and whispered to her friend Kelly.

"That bitch swear she the shit. I just wanted to see if that bitch would lie. Don't no big time baller want shit to do with that hood rat. Look at her, all she got is a big ass on her, and she looks okay. Her jeans don't fit like mine though." Michelle said slightly disgusted.

The thumping bass of rap music catches the ladies attention as they focused upon the continuous spinning rims on an all black tricked out 2011 Dodge Charger that pulled up in front of the salon. The women became more intrigued once the driver's door opened and a six foot, brown skinned brotha with a low haircut and well trimmed goatee stepped out. He was crisp and clean in his red Polo style shirt, black slacks, black shoes and Cartier glasses. He left his car running and walked into the salon. All eyes admirably followed his every step as he passed by.

"Damn baby, are you my husband?" Michelle asked as she flirted with the brotha.

"Not this time baby, I'm here for Cognac." He answered with a slight smirk as he glanced at Michelle then back at Cognac.

Michelle immediately looked over at Kelly and instantly went into hate mode.

"What? She must've paid this dude or promised him some phenomenal head tonight or something." Michelle leaned and uttered to Kelly. Kelly knew that Michelle was jealous and really wanted her to stop hating.

Cognac had no idea that Keith had come in. She was getting her area in order. Normally he doesn't make surprise visits, but since he just happened to be in the area he couldn't resist. He walked up to her admiring the way she was flexing and bending as she was cleaning her station.

"Damn baby you look so sexy wiping down your work area." Keith said with a smile.

Cognac looked up into the mirror and noticed Keith was behind her enjoying the view.

"Keith, hey baby. What brings you here, handsome?" Cognac asked as she turned around, walked up to him and hugged him.

"Thought me and you could do something spontaneous and go over to 1917 American Bistro restaurant for a little fine dining if you aint to busy today." Keith replied.

"Yes, that's fine. Actually I'm done for the day." Cognac said as she turned to go sit her cleaning supplies under the counter.

Regina couldn't help that she overheard their conversation, and politely interrupted.

"Hey cuz, what about Lyla? Doesn't she have a two o'clock appointment?" Regina asked.

"She was supposed to but she sent me a text message saying if she don't get a baby sitter she might not make it. I called her ass twice and she didn't answer her phone so I don't know what to tell her. If she didn't always cancel her appointments at the last minutes I would probably stay, but not this time." Cognac replied.

"Yeah, but what if she shows up? It aint even two o'clock yet." Regina said as she proceeded to do her clients hair.

"Yeah, but its close enough, she aint answering her phone, and I'm not about to put my day on hold waiting on her. Don't worry about it, Ima jus call Lyla and tell her she's going to have to reschedule her appointment because I have to go." Cognac said.

"Aye, well she did it to herself then." Regina said in a low calm manor.

Cognac looked to Keith and said "Baby, let me introduce you to my cousin I was telling you about. Regina this is Keith, and Keith this is my favorite big cousin in the world Regina." Cognac said.

"Hey Keith, nice to meet you." Regina said as she shook his hand.

"My pleasure to meet you, Miss Regina. I heard a lot about you." Keith said.

"Really? Don't believe a word of it. But seriously I've heard a lot about you as well." Regina replied.

Cognac could see Michelle and Kelly over there staring at them and talking. She knew that Michelle was hatin earlier and probably still was as they spoke. Cognac just smirked to herself and decided she was about to go change shirts.

"Well baby let me just run in the back real quick and we can go." Cognac said as she looked at Keith.

"Okay sexy do ya thing." Keith replied.

As Cognac walked into the back room to change, Regina figured she could pick Keith's brain and find out a little more about him.

"So um Keith, I heard you are quite a charmer." Regina said as she frequently looked back and forth at Keith, and her client.

"Well I aint gone say all that, but I'm a pretty cool brotha I'd say." Keith replied.

"That's wsup, so what do you do for a living?" Regina asked.

By that time Cognac returned and was ready to go. She figured Regina was probably being big cuz and was probably letting Keith have it; she gets that from Aunt Val.

"Okay Keith lets go baby, I'm hungry." Cognac said.

"Okay well it was nice to finally meet you Miss Regina." Keith said as he and Cognac turned and left to go to dinner.

"It was nice meeting you to, Keith. Y'all enjoy the day and be safe." Regina said as they were heading to the door.

"Alright boo I will call you later." Cognac replied.

Michelle just looked at Cognac and just couldn't keep her fucking mouth shut and mind her own business.

"Girl you gone have to teach me your secrets, cause I need a man." Michelle said to Cognac.

"I'm pretty sure you already know what you can do." Cognac replied as she walked on by.

Michelle just looked at her as Cognac walked towards the door and noticed the writing on the back of the shirt that Cognac had just put on. It read "Get A Life and Stop Hatin".

Michelle got a little stank ass look on her face as she uttered to herself "Bitch."

Kelly leaned over and said to Michelle "You do know that what you're doing right now is called hatin, right?"

Immediately Michelle took offence and just wanted to deny it although she knew inside she really was a envious bitch. However she replied. "Aint nobody hatin on that bitch! Learn what hatin is, then holla at me." Michelle said with a low-key attitude.

"Oh I know what hatin is, but you aint gotta get an attitude with me though." Kelly respectfully replied.

"Well I don't think you know what it is because if you did you wouldn't have said that to me." Michelle said with a little attitude.

"First of all I'm your girl so you aint gotta come on me like that! And just because you heated with her don't mean you gotta rub your attitude off on me." Kelly replied firmly.

"Well, learn what the fuck you talking about then." Michelle said in a very smart tone of voice.

"Oh I know what the fuck I'm talking about, but because you don't think I know what the fuck I'm talking about, let's ask somebody in here and see if they know what the fuck I'm talking about." Kelly suggested.

"I don't give a fuck, go ahead and make yourself look stupid." Michelle said nonchalantly as she sat back in her seat.

Kelly looked at Benita and got her attention. "Hey, excuse me what's your name?"

Benita looked at her and answered "Benita. You don't know as many times as you done been in here?" Benita asked.

"Yeah, I remember your face, just didn't remember your name." Kelly answered.

"It's all good boo, what's your question?" Benita asked as she continued doing hair.

"Okay look, Me and my girl was over here having a good discussion about what hatin is, and what it is that makes us women have such a hard time getting along with other women. To many times us sista's be hatin on each other for no reason and I would love to hear from some of you what you think hatin really is, and why it is active in our sistahood." Kelly asked as she sat down for someone else to take the floor and respond.

"Well, you're talking to the right one because I definitely got an answer for this one! The perfect example of what hatin is amongst us sista's is when a group of us women are out somewhere, let's say a club and another woman that's looking nothing less than very sexy walks in and the men are checking her out and trying to get at her. There's always some no-life having, jealous hearted bitch that aint got enough going on in her world who always got to try to find something negative to say about the woman instead of minding her own fuckin business.

She got to frown at the lady, and look her up and down with a lil funky attitude."

"Damn you really feeling this subject, huh? Hey, you were telling the truth though." Regina said as she chuckled.

"Hell yeah I'm feeling this subject because I can't stand these lame brauds that got to say negative remarks about a woman that aint said a damn thing wrong about her, or even did anything to her. I mean is life that miserable that you got to develop an attitude or a dislike towards somebody that aint did nothing to you?" Benita said with conviction.

"I'm feeling what you're saying because I had a friend that used to always try to find something about someone to degrade them about. I mean I would literally catch her ass just staring at other woman up and down just looking for something to say. I don't like that juvenile kiddy mess around me; I aint got time for it. Women need to grow the fuck up and stop all that jealousy." Regina replied.

"I know, right. Thank y'all sista's for proving my point." Kelly said.

Michelle looked at Kelly and asked. "So, you just gone put me on blast like that?"

"You the one said go ahead and ask them. Now you wanna complain about it because you didn't like the response? You can't even be real with yourself on no level, can you?" Kelly asked.

"I keeps it real all the time, flat out." Michelle said with a snarl on her face.

"Girl, save that bullshit for them flunky ass bitches that look up to that fronting ass shit you be doing. That shit don't impress me." Kelly said as she stood up.

"First of all bitch, you aint bout to keep talking shit to me!" Michelle said as she stood up, stepping out into the middle of the floor.

"Bitch, who you calling a bitch?!!" Kelly said, walking up on her just as Antonio had to step in between them.

"Ladies, calm down please?" Antonio asked.

"Look, I aint got time for this childish bullshit. Antonio, I will just reschedule my appointment for another day." Kelly expressed.

"That's cool, just call me and let me know when you want to reschedule." Antonio replied, just wanting to eradicate any drama.

"Okay." Kelly replied and left.

Antonio took a deep breath and just shook his head. Damn, cant we all just be civilized and get along?...

1917 AMERICAN BISTRO, Bon Appétit

7:37pm the classy sound of Detroit's own phenomenal band, **CONSCIOUS MINDS** serenaded the crowd at 1917 AMERICAN BISTRO. A poet by the name of **Omari King Wise** was gracing the audience with his lyrics as he flowed perfectly with the music. The lighting and ambience was relaxing and the hospitality of the waiters and waitresses was topnotch. The entrée of the day is one of their signature dishes, Blackened Catfish and two sides of your choice, Bon Appétit.

"I had so much fun at that **Khem Kemistry** concert. Thank you so much for taking me, sweetie." Cognac said as she sipped her glass of white merlot.

"You're very welcome, sexy. How does the catfish taste?" Keith asked as he sipped his Belvedere and cranberry.

"It is the bomb, you gotta taste it. How are your lamb chops and salmon?" Cognac asked.

"A.1 and this Fettuccine Alfredo is setting it off." Keith replied as he placed a fork full in his mouth.

"It looks delicious."

"Almost delicious as you taste."

"Freak." She replied with a nasty smirk.

"And? You like every bit of this freak to."

Cognac smiled as she sipped her wine "So, and?" Cognac replied sarcastically.

"I got your **SO** right here." Keith replied, clutching his crotch under the table.

"Boy, don't nobody want that little ass thang." Cognac retorted with the corners of her lips tightened.

"Whatever, keep talking." Keith said.

"You aint gone do nothing." Cognac replied.

"You lucky we in this restaurant because you'll be getting fucked on this table right now." Keith impressed.

Cognac and Keith were going back and forth in their freakish conversation when suddenly interrupted by the waitress "Hey, you two okay over here? You want any dessert or something else to drink?" The waitress asked with a smile.

"No, I'm fine." Cognac answered.

"I'll take one more of the Belve." Keith requested.

"Okay, I'll be right back." The waitress said and went back to place his order.

Everyone clapped as Omari King Wise and Conscious Minds finished an astounding performance. The host, Steven Sparrow Oneal walked back up to the stage and engaged the crowd. Everyone was feeling good and ready for more so he gladly introduced the next artist and her band.

"Ladies and Gentlemen, can you please put your hands together for *Zjai Renai* and *Soul Nation*!!!" *Sparrow* announced emphatically as the audience clapped and embraced them.

The band got situated, the drummer started the song off and the rest of the band followed beautifully. Zjai Renai hummed along with the melody and then captivated the crowd with her gorgeous voice and lyrics.

"She is good." Cognac expressed as her attention was drawn to the stage.

"I know. What did he say her name was, Zjai Renai or something like that?" Keith asked as he nodded his head to the melody.

"Yeah, it's Zjai Renai. That's a pretty name; it sounds classy."

"Right, I know. Hey look, I've been thinking...we've been seeing each other pretty much since New Years, I think you're smart, and sexy. In other words um, how you feel about being my woman?" Keith asked.

Cognac looked a little caught off guard as she paused and took a sip of her drink. She cleared her throat and then replied.

"I've been thinking about that. I think you're handsome, charming and pretty smart yourself. The only problem is I have a son, and I'll have a man who's a drug dealer. That automatically endangers our lives; I mean Lord forbid, but me or my son can get killed because somebody got it out for you. I want a husband... a husband I can grow old with. A husband who has a regular job and wants to be a positive role model to my son. Am I worth that to you?" Cognac asked.

Keith paused and looked around for a brief second and looked back at her and replied "Yes, you are definitely worth that to me. I know I can't keep living this way, and I do want to be married and have a family. I got a daughter, you've got a son and I don't want anything to happen to neither one of them. I'll tell you what, I'll let go of the drug game and flip real-estate. I got enough money put away to take care of us and invest in these properties and get them in good condition and sell them." Keith impressed.

"Sounds good, and I hope you mean what you say. I'm not going to say yes or no right now, and I hope that you respect my wishes and just show me that you mean what you say. And then I'll say yes as long as you act right." Cognac expressed with a slight smile.

"You've got a deal." Keith replied.

This day couldn't have ended more perfect. It was a gorgeous sunny day, and the temperature was just right, Eighty-two degrees with a nice breeze. Got off work early, changed cloths, the **Khem Kemistry** concert at **Chene Park** was off the hook. Then they closed out the evening with some fine dining and fantastic entertainment over at **1917 AMERICAN BISTRO**.

And Then There Was...Demarco

11:08pm Cognac had just got in not too long ago after having a fabulous time with Keith. She couldn't wait to get out of her cloths and slip into something more comfortable and did just that. She wore a pink and white fitted tank top and a pair of pink boy shorts with two numbers written in white on the front and the back that read **69**. She stood in the bathroom mirror brushing her teeth for a few minutes when her cell phone rang. She glanced at it and saw that it was Regina. She took her toothbrush out her mouth then picked the phone up and muttered "Hold on" with a mouth full of toothpaste and spit.

"What? I can't hear you. It sounds like you got something thick in your mouth." Regina said, being funny about Cognac's muffled words.

Cognac turned the water on in the face bowl, bent over and cupped some water into her mouth and swished it around. She spit it out and then got on the phone.

"Wdup, NIGGA!" Cognac said, very amped.

"Uhg girl that sounded nasty as hell." Regina responded.

"What? I had to spit." Cognac replied.

"Yeah, but what was you doing right before I called that made you have to spit?" Regina asked, sarcastically.

"The same thing you love to do, give some good head, catch that nut in ya mouth, and spit it out." Cognac answered sarcastically.

"Well, they say it helps cure breast cancer if you swallow." Regina said, being funny.

"Eeeeewwww Regina, you aint supposed to say that, take that back." Cognac replied.

"You right, okay I take it back." Regina responded in a coy manner.

"But no, I was just brushing my teeth. What you up to?" Cognac asked as she walked back into her kitchen, grabbed a bottle of water out of the refrigerator and sat down at the table in her kitchen-net.

"Nothing, just chillin, watching the news. But wait; tell me how the concert went. Was **Khem Kemistry** throwing down?!!" Regina asked, very excited.

"Yes girl, he was the bomb as usual. I mean Regina, it was live. I had so much fun." Cognac impressed joyfully.

"That's wsup cuz, I'm so happy you enjoyed yourself. What else yall do?" Regina asked.

"After the concert we got something to drink and cruised around **Belle Isle** a couple of times, enjoying the breeze. Then we drove back over on the Westside and got something to eat at **1917 AMERICAN BISTRO**." Cognac said as she peeked out of her living room window thinking that she has heard something.

"That is so wsup, cuz. Wait a minute...what the hell?!" Regina blurted out.

"What's the matter?" Cognac asked, concerned.

"Girl, I'm sitting here looking at this news, and some dude just killed his ex girlfriend and new boyfriend because she broke up with him and posted it on one of them internet sites." Regina said.

"What, which one?!" Cognac asked, shaking her head.

"I don't even remember, I think it was MyFace or FaceSpace, one of them two." Regina said.

Cognac laughed her ass off.

"Hold up, I aint laughing at the incident, I'm laughing at you because you got it all crossed up. It's obvious that you don't have a page, because that aint the name of either one of them." Cognac replied, still laughing.

"That's okay, laugh all you want but that's why I don't get on that stuff. People be seeing all your business, and stalking you. It provides too many avenues to cheat in relationships and get in trouble." Regina said.

"I hear you but on some real talk, it's all up to the individual and how they use that site. I use it to promote my business; I don't try to date nobody on there at all. People ask me why I have all those friends on my page if I don't know them and I simply tell them that it's because I'm trying to promote my business to everybody, not just people I know. And if somebody wants to get on there and use it as a dating site that's on them; you can't blame everybody for other people's actions. It will be absolutely dumb to not promote your business on there based off other people's juvenile intentions or somebody's misunderstanding of it." Cognac stressed.

"You right, I feel you, you can't blame everybody for some peoples actions. Eeww hold up!! The news just said that the lady broke up with her boyfriend and she posted on her page. The new dude that she had started seeing got on there and made a comment and the ex-boyfriend saw it and he got on there and responded. They both got to arguing back and forth and making threats. Later on that night he came over and shot them both, and killed them."

"Damn, that is messed up. This type of stuff makes me scared to get into a relationship now days. If you wanna break up with somebody it's a consequence behind it." Cognac said as she sat up, thinking about her situation with Demarco and Keith.

Cognac knew she was playing with fire by dating both, Keith, and Demarco. She couldn't help that she was sort of starting to like Keith a little more. Demarco had recently said a couple of things to her during a conversation that were questionable, and made her decide she wanted to back off from him. She was concerned about his violent behavior and his lack of respect for women at times. She was also still bitter from her previous relationship with Marcello because she gave her all and he betrayed her. That's why she made it up in her mind that she would heartlessly get whatever she could get out of these dudes. However it's hard to remain bitter when you're a naturally loving person, but when you're trapped in the duality of love and hate it's a great possibility the outcome of your decision making will be regretful...and sometimes FATAL.

"Hey, with all this relationship drama going on out here I gotta ask. What's going with you and Demarco? It seemed like you liked him more than Keith at first but now it seems to be the other way around." Regina asked out of curiosity.

"I mean...I don't know, it's like I didn't really care which one of them I was hanging out with at first. Initially I wasn't letting no nigga get close to me like that anyway, but...lately I've been sort of digging Keith. And as far as Demarco goes, he's been on some ole stalking me type shit, calling me, texting me, questioning me about who I with, and where I'm at? I had to tell him a couple of times that we aint on that type of level. He act like were in a relationship. I think I'm about to stop fucking with him all together if he don't chill out with all that shit." Cognac said, shaking her head.

"I hear you boo, but...you gotta remember you are getting money from these guys and accepting gifts from them. Whether we like it or not aint nobody out here giving up something for nothing. If somebody's breaking you off some money and buying you stuff they feel like you're theirs or you owe them something. We might say that's crazy or that aint how it's supposed to be but when you look at how things are going out here we gotta start respecting people's feelings more. People will kill you and then kill themselves before they allow you to get what they got then say to hell with them and then go be with somebody else." Regina replied sincerely.

"You know, sometimes it amazes me how you got to be so wise at a young age. You sound just like Uncle Gary or Ms. Sarah Langston sometimes." Cognac asked.

"I don't know, you might be right; trust me I've had my share of lectures from them both. But I've also learned from experience, and I don't want you to make the same mistakes I did."

"Thank you, cuz. You've always been in my corner, and I love you for that." Cognac said

"Well look, I'm about to get up off of this phone, eat something, and lie down and go to bed. I got an early start tomorrow. "Regina said, yawning.

"Okay bay, well I'll see you tomorrow." Cognac replied.

"Oh wait! I just wanna say Happy Birthday."

"Thank you boo, even though it aint my birthday just yet."

"I know, I just wanted to say it first." Regina said and laughed.

"Aww thank you boo." Cognac said and smiled.

"You welcome cuz. Alright boo, Ima get off this phone and I'll see you tomorrow."

"Alright girl, bye." Cognac said as they hung up.

Cognac sat the phone down on her thigh and lied back on the couch. She was exhausted from work, motherly duties, and the sometimes overwhelming stress and drama that had been going on in her life over the last eight or nine months. She could feel the excessive tightness in her muscles in the back of her neck, shoulders, and mid back. She closed her eyes and exhaled as she laid there getting some well needed quiet time. After five minutes she started drifting off. Unfortunately her phone rang and woke her out of her sleep. She opened her eyes in disbelief and sighed. Who the fuck can it be now?! Can I please get some fucking rest, she thought to herself as she looked at the caller I.D. As if the stress couldn't get any worse, Demarco calls. She sighed slightly and continued lying back on the couch and let the call go to voicemail. A minute later Demarco called again, and she let it go to voicemail. Once again stressful thoughts interrupted her sleep as she just lied there starring at the ceiling in disbelief. She knew she was going to have to let Demarco know that she wasn't feeling him anymore but she wanted to spring it on him in the right way. Right then was the wrong time because she was sleepy as hell and knew that he would demand an explanation, or perhaps act a fool and she definitely was in no mood to argue or deal with any drama.

Essential Beauty Salon

Today the sun couldn't have shinned brighter. The temperature was a gorgeous eighty-two degrees, mild humidity with the perfect breeze; damn...this has to be what paradise really feels like. Days like these everybody's feeling good, and got their clothes crisp and clean. People trying to be seen and trust me, aint a woman finna let this beautiful day go by and her hair aint whipped. As usual Essential Beauty Salon was in the business of beautifying women and they were doing it very well. Inside, the sound of stainless steel scissors snipped through the air every time the blades clipped split ends asymmetrically. Across the room, Benita was focused with a sharp eye, and steady hand as the edge of a razor arched a woman's eyebrows to perfection. And of course what's a day at Essential Beauty Salon without the...Topic of Discussion?

"Girl, you have a serious case of split ends going on here but when I'm done you gone be on point." Regina said to her client, Ms. Sinclair.

"Gina, you always have me looking fly when I leave here. That's why I love coming to you." Sinclair replied as she noticed her cell phone ringing.

She asked Regina to hold up a second so she could look and see who was calling. She reached down and grabbed her purse off of the floor, and then stuck her hand inside and took her phone out. It was her husband, Ronald calling so she answered. Ronald never said anything and instinctively she said hello two more times, and again Ronald never said a word. She was about to hang up but was slightly alarmed by the muffled sounds and voices she heard. With an inquisitive look on her face she tuned out everything that was going on around her and listened closely. **WHAT THE FUCK**, she thought to herself as her heartbeat accelerated and flames slowly shot through her veins like lava. She hoped she was just misunderstanding the sounds coming through the phone, but unfortunately she wasn't. What she heard was flat out undeniable; somebody was getting fucked. What she didn't know was that on the other end of the phone it was her husband at home jacking off like a muthafucka as he watched an intense porno scene on DVD called Baby

Got Booty 33. In the process of rapidly beating the fingerprints off his right hand he accidentally hit the call button on his phone and it dialed Sinclair. All Sinclair knew was that she heard somebody fucking and she was about to nut up.

"Ronald...Ronald...**MUTHAFUCKA   I KNOW YOU HEAR ME**!!" Sinclair said loudly, forgetting where she was.

In the process of concentrating on the juicy, round, plump ass on the screen, and squirting all on the towel he carefully placed across his stomach he heard Sinclair's voice. Immediately he looked around like **WHAT THE HELL** then glanced at his phone and saw Sinclair was on, listening. Quickly he grabbed the remote with his left hand and hit pause and with his jack off hand he grabbed the phone and answered it.

"Hey baby! What's going on?" Ronald answered as he jumped with a nasty look on his face after getting a little cum on his jaw from off of his hand.

"Don't hey baby me, muthafucka! What the hell is going on over there is the question?!" Sinclair asked seriously.

"Baby, what, what you talking about?" Ronald asked nervously as he unconsciously whipped the nut off of his jaw with the cum catch towel.

"Why the hell you stuttering, Ronald?! Why you stuttering? I heard you over there fucking some bitch and then got all quiet when you heard my voice!" Sinclair said as she stood up.

"Baby, aint nobody here but me!!" Ronald replied sincerely yet nervous as his heart fluttered.

"So you trying to say I'm hearing things now? I heard that bitch moaning when you accidentally called me, I aint stupid!!" Sinclair stressed.

"Baby I swear aint nobody here but me! What you heard was this." Ronald stressed as he hit play on the remote.

The sounds of sex, voices and moaning set Sinclair on fire! She thought Ronald was maliciously fucking somebody while she listened on the phone.

"Ooohh you trying to get fucked up, huh! You trying to get your little ding-a-ling shot the fuck off, huh?!" Sinclair asked furiously.

"Baby, you kind of sound like Juvenile. You know, that rap dude." Ronald said.

"**MUTHAFUCKA**, do you think I'm in a juvenile rapping mood? What I'm think about doing to your ass sound more like prison if you ask me. But I see you got balls and jokes, huh? Ronald, you gone cheat on me and rub it in my face like that?" Sinclair asked with her fist balled up tightly.

"**NO, NO BABY I'M NOT CHEATING**, that's **Baby Got Booty 33** you hear playing in the DVD player." Ronald admitted.

"Baby Got Booty 33?" Sinclair asked with an incredulous look on her face.

"Yeah, Baby Got Booty 33. You know, the porno DVD?" Ronald said, chuckling a little bit.

Sinclair paused for a second and then asked "Ronald, you cheating on me with a damn porno flick?"

"Cheating? How is that cheating?" Ronald asked in a piercing high pitch voice.

Sinclair's frustration showed as she exhaled, and hung up the phone. She regained her focus and realized all eyes were on her....you could hear a pin drop at that moment. She looked around and said "Sorry, I caught my man cheating, flatout." Everyone just kind of looked at her in amazement as she stood there looking baffled and asked "What? Y'all do know what cheating is, right?" Sinclair asked, wondering why everyone was just looking at her with their mouths open in disbelief.

Sinclair sat down and Benita replied "Yeah, I know what cheating is, and I know what the good book say; Thou should not commit adultery. But in defense of the porno flick watchers it never said Thou couldn't watch a DVD of people fucking. If anything they're the ones sinning, not you. Naw, I don't think that's cheating, boo." Benita said, stirring the new topic of the day.

"How is that not cheating?" Sinclair asked, sort of staggered by Benita's reply.

"Because cheating is when you are having an physical affair with another person; you can't fuck a DVD. That's just... watching sex. And even if he did decide to fuck the DVD by sticking his dick through that hole in the middle of it, it still aint cheating." Benita answered.

"So a man thinketh so it is in his heart." Sinclair quoted.

"So now we reading minds and judging thoughts? Don't you know that if we start reading minds and penalize each other for it we'll be getting divorces, whooping asses, and going to jail every thirty seconds?" Benita said, very animatedly.

"I kind of agree with Benita. How can it be cheating if you don't have an actual person you're cheating with?" Regina asked.

"Because it is; he shouldn't be looking at or thinking about no other woman's ass but mines." Sinclair said sincerely.

"Are you serious?" Regina asked.

"Yes, I'm dead serious. I would hope that you wouldn't want your man looking at another woman in a lustful manner either." Sinclair replied.

"You don't think that's a little unrealistic and too much to be worrying about?" Regina asked.

"Why do you think it's unrealistic?" Sinclair asked with a slight incredulous look on her face.

"Because it's unrealistic to think that you or your mate will go through the day and not look at other people; that's impossible. You'll be lying to yourself if you said that you didn't look at other people." Regina answered.

"Whatever, you know what I'm talking about." Sinclair retorted.

"Okay, let's get a man's point of view. Antonio, do you think watching porno's and masturbating is cheating?" Regina asked, looking over at Antonio.

Antonio felt like all eyes were on him because he was in a room full of women wanting to hear his reply. He looked around, shook his head and smiled, feeling like a rabbit in the middle of a pack of lions waiting for him to make the wrong move.

"Damn, you just gone pull me in y'all convo and throw me to the wolves, huh?" Antonio asked as he continued giving his client a pedicure.

"Boy, aint nobody gone bite you...well I take that back, cause they might wanna bite you in a good way, but um...just answer the damn question!" Benita said very animated.

"Well, technically it aint cheating because you're not physically with somebody else. And as far as the mental part of it, that's God's area right there because only God can read a person's thoughts without assumption and being wrong. However, as far as looking at somebody goes...Regina is right, you are always going to see people where ever you go, and you're going to be attracted to some of them, but it's all about how you react in that situation." Antonio answered.

"A woman's intuition is never wrong. I know when my man is lusting after something he see's." Sinclair replied.

"Whatever, back in the day maybe that was true, but now days... people's emotions are so out of whack they don't truly know the difference between intuition and assumption. And because of that it ultimately leads to false accusation, divorce and break-ups when it don't have to be that way." Antonio replied.

"Well, it's an exception to the rule in my case, because I know I'm right." Sinclair replied, stubbornly.

"You only know because you have conclusive evidence. You heard the DVD playing so that's the only reason why you truly knew. But before he made a mistake and called you, you never even knew he was playing a DVD. So what's that say for your intuition?" Antonio stated very well.

Sinclair scoffed at Antonio's remarks and replied "Well my man better gawk at me or stair at the ground the whole time if he know what's good for him."

"Whew, I bet your man is a nervous wreck. In about two years he gone be looking like Moses after he got done talking to that burning bush." Antonio said, being funny about her demanding personality.

"Man, enough of all the who looking at who talk; y'all getting too far off the subject for me. Bottom line is masturbating and watching porno's cheating? I say it aint, you aint gotta worry about your mate catching shit and giving you STD's. It also adds to your sex life if you're into freaky shit like me. And matter of fact it will teach some of y'all non freaky, boring in the bedroom asses how to please your man and turn him on. It's a win, win situation." Benita stressed.

"Preach Benita, preach! I'm loving what you're saying right now." Antonio added.

"A man wants his woman to be a freak, not some nerd that thinks freaky and nasty shit is bad. They don't want to hear somebody say oh it's nasty, it taste nasty, **THEY HATE THAT SHIT!** They want to hear their woman say boo, let me suck your dick while you're driving, or before you go to work, or when he come in from work. And if you're the bomb like me you'll suck his dick every Sunday while he's watching the football game. Now I'm done preaching." Benita said eloquently as all the women looked at her like they can't believe that she actually said that shit. The women may not have said shit but they definitely took note and planned on trying it themselves when they get home to their men.

However, just outside in front of the salon a bunch of laughter and screaming was catching people's attention as a mother and her four children had gotten out of a car. Their ages were eight, six, four, and three with the oldest being a boy, the six year old being a girl, and the two youngest were boys. The two youngest were fighting and yelling at each other by the car. The four year old started chasing the three year old around the car and into the middle of the parking lot just as a Black Chrysler Ram pickup truck was approaching. The squeal of rubber burning across the concrete as the truck was braking to avoid hitting the children causing an unpleasant scene.

"Get y'all asses back over here before I beat the fuckin shit y'all!" Veronica yelled as she rushed over and snatched them both by the arm and pulled them back over to her car.

The people in the truck shook their heads pitifully as they carefully drove pass the trifling mom and her children. Inside the salon the people were shocked and petrified as they looked on at what could've been a hideous child fatality. Regina closed her eyes, shook her head and exhaled slowly; just glad that there was no tragedy.

"Aw damn, here come Veronica and the children of the corn." Antonio said, being sarcastic and funny.

"You wrong for that, all children are beautiful." Regina said, trying not to laugh too much at his remark.

"Whatever, you know what I'm talking about. You see she couldn't get a babysitter, they would've charged her double, and she would've had to throw in a pint of liquor just so the babysitter can cope." Antonio retorted humorously.

"What she needs to do is feed them kids some ham sandwiches and Nyquil before she bring them up here with her!" Benita said very amped.

Regina and a few others busted out laughing. Regina had to gather herself the best she could as she tried to get out what she was trying to say. "Benita, you are a fool! What the hell is ham sandwiches and Nyquil gone do?"

"It's gone balance their little behinds out! After eating some thick ass ham sandwiches and a couple of swigs of Nyquil they will be sleeping they ass off while she get her hair done. By time they wake up it'll be time for them to go." Benita stated.

Everybody laughed and said their hilarious remarks and then got quiet or switched their conversation just as Veronica and her children walked through the door. Veronica told her children to sit down in the empty seats in the seating area just as you walk in. She walked over to talk to Peaches who was getting ready to do her hair, but didn't know her four year old was following right behind her. Peaches knew Veronica from elementary school, and they just so happen to run into each other later on in their lives. Peaches let Veronica know that she was a professional hairstylist and Veronica would come to her whenever she got the money to treat herself. However, during their brief conversation her four year old was tapping her on the thigh trying to get her to pick him up. The six year old and the four year old had gotten out of their seats and started roaming around the salon. They started getting in the way of Antonio and Benita while they were working on their clients. The only one that remained seated was the eight year old who was embarrassed because his mother just let's his sister and brother's do what they want to do. Antonio and Benita both looked at each other then at

Veronica wondering when she would say something to her children and make them sit down. Benita wanted to say something so bad to the little girl but she felt the more respectable thing to do was let their mother address the situation, so she got the mothers attention.

"Excuse me, Veronica I don't want your children to get hurt by being over here in the work area. Can you please make them sit down over there in the waiting area?" Benita politely asked.

Veronica was one of those parents that feel like they're just kids, they're not hurting anybody. But she wasn't trying to let her ghetto fabulous side out so she told her children to sit down and turned around and finished talking to Peaches. The children heard her but ignored her and kept meddling and being in the way. Regina, De'Juan, Antonio, Benita, and even the clients were looking around at each other as they curiously waited to see if Veronica was going to get her troublesome children and make them sit down. All while Veronica was talking her three year old was steadily tapping her on the thigh and crying asking her to pick him up. Veronica excused herself from talking to Peaches so that she could go to the restroom to pee. She took her three year old with her but left the other children still out there undisciplined and getting all in the way. They couldn't believe that Veronica just walked off without at least making her children sit down first. Benita politely asked the little girl to stop touching the hair products and go sit down in her seat. Antonio had enough and decided to say something to the little boy who was also getting in peoples way and surly on their nerves. "Hey, little man. Excuse me little man, you hear me talking to you." Antonio said getting the little boys attention. The little boy just paused for a second and answered "What?"

"Go sit down like your Mother told you to do and stop being hard headed. You can get hurt messing around over here." Antonio said kindly to the little boy.

"You not my Daddy." The little boy replied with a smart mouth.

By that time Veronica was on her way back from the restroom her four year ran up to her and lied, saying that Antonio was hollering and being mean to him. Veronica got a slight attitude and walked up to address Antonio.

"Um Sir, don't holler at my kids, thank you." Veronica said in a very testy manner.

"Woman, I aint said nothing wrong to your kids, I just kindly ask him to go sit down. They can get hurt playing around in here." Antonio replied.

"Mam, aint nobody hollered at your kids but it would be nice if you would get your children and make them sit down." Regina said, firmly.

Just as Veronica turned around to reply to Regina she heard her daughter crying. She immediately turned back around and saw her on the floor. She had tripped and fell, hurting her elbow on the ground. Benita shook her head as she helped the little girl to her feet. The children had finally gotten on Veronica's last nerve so she made it up in her mind that she would just reschedule her appointment and take her children home.

"I don't know what you shaking your head for." Veronica said with a nasty look on her face as she glanced at Benita and then grabbed her daughter by the arm.

"Something sorry and pathetic." Benita replied, looking directly at Veronica.

"I know you aint referring to me." Veronica retorted, pulling her daughter along.

"If the shoe fits wear it." Benita said in slight sarcasm.

"Peaches, I'm sorry Ima have to reschedule my appointment. I hope you not mad." Veronica asked.

"Naw you good, I know you have to tend to the little babies" Peaches replied.

"Y'all come on!" Veronica said as she held the door open for her children as they walked out.

The energy in the salon was baffling. The people shook their heads and exhaled in disbelief. Of course people had their personal comments and opinions about the way Veronica handled her children. Everything went back to normal as Regina and everybody continued beautifying their clients. Being that Veronica walked out Peaches cleaned her area and took her a slight break. Benita...well, is always going to be Benita; caring, down to earth and silly as hell with a bunch of jokes.

"Antonio, why you let your Wifee come up in here like that?" Benita asked, being funny.

"Trust me; she couldn't even make it to girlfriend status. I aint dealing with no woman who aint got control over her kids. That's too much of a damn headache. I aint saying that kids have to be perfect or aint going to get into shit, but damn you gotta discipline them when their getting off the hook." Antonio replied as he added gorgeous detail to his client's fingernails.

"I feel you because I damn sho aint dealing with no man like that either. Bottom line, have your kids under control or I'm out the door.

In the mean time while everyone was voicing their opinions Peaches decided she was going to take the rest of the day off. She grabbed her purse from her locker in the backroom and walked into the restroom. She grabbed her brush out of her purse and brushed her hair to her liking. She put some lip gloss on her lips, then put her shades on, and walked out feeling like a star. She said bye to everyone and stopped just as she was walking out of the door when Regina said something to her.

"Aye, don't forget its Coney's surprise party over Aunt Val's so make sure you there." Regina said.

"What time?" Peaches asked.

"Eight o'clock." Regina replied.

"Okay, just call me around six-thirty."

"Alright, will do."

"Alright." Peaches said and left.

Aunt Valerie's House

"Eric, get off that X station and help me get things together for your momma's birthday party lil boy. Now I don't want to have to keep telling you." Valerie said from the kitchen where she was picking and washing some Mustard and Turnip Greens for the party.

"Here I go, Auntie." Eric said as he darted into the kitchen.

Valerie smiled then gave him a kiss on the forehead and said "You know you auntie sweetie pie and I love you, but if you don't get your tail out there in that yard, Ima get me one of them switches off the tree and whoop the skin off ya behind. You hear me? I've been asking you all day, now." Aunt Val said, you could hear that she wasn't joking although she said it in a nice tone of voice.

"But Auntie." Eric said with a sulky expression, and a slouching body.

"But Auntie nothing, I need you to get out there and clean up with no lip. Now you don't want me to tell your Uncle Mike that I've had to tell you over and over about getting out there and cleaning up that yard. And you and I both know he work out every day all day too. He bench press about eight-hundred pounds, he curl five-hundred pounds per bicep, and if he get a hold to you with one of them heroic mighty hands he gone beat you like the Passion of the Christ. Now if you're smart you'll get out there and get to cleaning up that yard. You hear me?" Valerie said as she pointed at Eric with a hand full of collard greens.

"Yes I hear you Auntie, but I did clean up the yard." Eric said.

Valerie looked outside through the kitchen window at her yard, and still saw toys and miscellaneous things on the lawn. Then she looked across the street at Mr. Seymore's yard and said "What you do? You cleaned Mr. Seymore's yard across the street? Because I know you aint talking about this yard in front of my house, Eric. Come here and look at all this stuff on this lawn. You got basketballs, footballs, candy wrappers and stuff all on the grass."

"Okay Auntie, I'm sorry. I'm about to do it now." Eric said in a disheartened voice after feeling like he let Auntie down.

Valerie loved Eric with all her heart; he was like the son she'd never had. She wanted him to be an honorable young man that's why she stayed on him so. Whenever she'd want him to understand a lesson she'd thoroughly explain it to him so he'd understand it fluently. Eric grabbed a couple of garbage bags from out of the pantry, and just as he got ready to walk out of the door she stopped him.

"Eric, before you go out there let Auntie tell you something. I stay on you about doing things in a firm way because I love you and I want you to grow up to be a great man. I try to teach you great qualities that you will need to apply to yourself to help you be that great man one day. So when you get older and have a wife and children, you will know how to take care of them and be the head of your household like a King is suppose to be. I refuse to have you grow up like some of these other little boys out here that have no understanding of what life is all about. I don't want you out there standing on the corner selling drugs killing off your own black race for a dollar. I don't want the police coming to get you and locking you up, or finding you lying in the street dead... I don't want to see another mother come to her own child's funeral...that's not the way it's supposed to be. I want you to be a great man and lead your people from this psychological warfare in which we live. I know you're only a young man right now but greatness doesn't start when you become a grown man. Greatness is instilled in you from youth like a seed planted in the earth. Life will provide you with lessons that will help your knowledge grow the same way sunlight and rain does a rose. You understand?" Aunt Val asked.

"Yes, Auntie?"

"Good, now go ahead out there and fix that yard up while Auntie prepares this food. Okay sweetie?" Aunt Val asked.

"Okay Auntie" said Eric as he walked out the door. Immediately Eric turned around and walked back in the door. He walked up to Auntie and tapped her on the side.

"Hey Auntie."

"Yes Eric, what do you need young fella?" Valerie asked as she picked the greens.

"I just wanted to tell you thank you for always teaching me like you do." Eric said.

"Thank you sweetie, that was very nice of you to say. You still gotta get out there and clean up that yard though." Valerie replied, hoping Eric didn't think he'd gotten out of cleaning up by saying some sweet words.

"But you were wrong about one thing, Auntie." Eric stated.

"Oh yeah, and what was that lil boy?" Aunt Val asked as she looked at him with an eyebrow raised.

"Earlier I heard you call my game an X-Station. It's called an Xbox, not an X station." Eric replied with a smile.

"Mmmm Hhmmm, is that so? Well I don't care what "X" it is. Xbox, X station, an EX girlfriend, I don't give a rat's behind if it's the XGames. But what I do know is if you don't get that yard done, Ima mark a big X on that video game and then it's gonna be Ex-stinct. You hear me?" Valerie asked.

"Yes Auntie." Eric answered as he turned and walked outside with the quickness to straighten up the yard.

A silver 2010 Chevy Malibu pulled up in front of the house. A coffee brown-skinned sista with short pretty locks stepped out from the driver's seat. She saw Eric and walked over to him.

"Hey cousin, Reonna." Eric said as he stood there with the garbage bag in his hand and a smile on his face.

"Hey, little Eric. Where's Aunt Val at?" Reonna asked as she leaned over and gave him a hug.

"She's in the house cooking." Eric answered.

"Your Momma here?" Reonna asked.

"Nall, she gone." Eric answered.

"Okay sweetie, tell her I came by here looking for her." Reonna said as she walked up to the front door.

"Okay." Eric replied as he continued straightening up the yard.

"Knock, knock Reonna said as she opened the front door and entered. The pleasurable smell of good ole soul food made her mouth water as she entered the kitchen. She walked over to the stove and saw a huge industrial size pot of greens cooking. She bent down and looked through the oven window and saw macaroni baking in one dish and cornbread in another. She shook her head as she stood up thinking to herself how she wanted to eat the hell out of that food!

"Aunt Val." Reonna called out.

"Who is that?" Val asked from the other room.

"It's Reonna." Reonna answered.

Seconds later Aunt Val came easing around the corner with a smile.

"Is that my, Reonna?" Valerie asked excitingly with her arms open.

Reonna just smiled like a big kid, all teeth and gums as Aunt Val hugged her. All the children in the family loved Aunt Val because she always made them all feel good.

"Dang Auntie, you always got it smelling good in the kitchen." Reonna said as she kissed Val on the cheek.

"You know Auntie gotta feed y'all and gotta do it right. Oh, and I'm making your favorite." Valerie replied as she lifted the top on the greens and gave them a stir with her stirring spoon.

"Aw Auntie, you making shrimp pasta salad?" Reonna asked very animated and exited.

"I sure am." Aunt Val replied with a smile.

"Auntie, please put me a big bowl to the side, because you know me and Cognac WILL be fighting over your pasta salad." Reonna asked.

"Cognac? Well in that case I don't think you need to be drinking if you think it's going to have you fighting, sweetie. That just don't make no sense." Aunt Val said with an incredulous look on her face.

Reonna laughed and replied "No, I aint talking about a drink Auntie, I'm talking about Rachelle. You know Rachelle's nickname is Cognac." Reonna answered.

"Oh yeah, then what's your nickname, Christian Brother's? Paul Mason or something?" Aunt Val asked, being funny.

"Hecky nall, Auntie! You are funny." Reonna replied, laughing.

"Hey, I'm just checking." Aunt Val replied.

"But for real, Auntie put me a big bowl to the side, please?" Reonna asked.

"Don't worry I'm going to make a huge bowl of it, more than enough." Valerie replied.

"And speaking of Cognac, oops I mean Rachelle. Where is she at anyway?" Reonna asked.

"I don't know, she's either up at the shop or out with that Keith guy." Valerie said, not sounding too flattered by the thought.

"Keith? Who is that?" Reonna asked.

"Some guy she met back somewhere around Christmas. I aint too sure about him; I think he's one of them street thugs, but I can't tell her who to date and who not to date." Valerie said.

"Oh, well...I got somebody with me I would like her to meet, to bad she aint here. He's handsome, intelligent, seems to be a gentleman. He works, I mean he's pretty much what a good woman is looking for." Reonna impressed.

"I really wish Rachelle would give one of these good men a try and stop messing around with these street runners." Aunt Val said as she shook her head while fantasizing and wishing.

"She will Auntie, don't worry. Well look, Ima go because I got my boyfriend and his friend outside in the car. I don't want to be inconsiderate and just keep them sitting out there waiting." Reonna said as she kissed Val on the cheek.

"Okay, well I'll see you later on tonight at the party." Valerie said.

"Okay Auntie, love you." Reonna said as she walked to the door.

"Okay, I love you to." Aunt Val said as she looked through the kitchen window and smiled as Reonna hugged Eric and then got in her car and pulled off.

The Jack of Hearts

With a mean scowl and a bleak lost stare on his face, Demarco sat there on his living room couch holding his phone wondering why Cognac wasn't answering his calls. Despite the fact that he and Cognac had never became a couple he still felt like she owed him more. He felt like she owed him more than just ignoring him or just playing him like he was just another nigga she was dating. He felt like he should be the top nigga in her life and she should consider him before any dude she was fucking around with. She should and answer his calls no matter who the fuck she was in front of!! He unlocked his touch screen with the swipe of his finger then opened the call log and redialed Cognac. He couldn't believe that he kept getting her fucking voicemail! Just the thought of all the money he's spent on her, wining and dining her ass, and buying her nice things was pissing him the fuck off, because she didn't appreciate him and the shit he did for her. He tossed his phone down on the couch and picked up a pack of cigarettes that was sitting on the end-table. He tapped the pack upside down on his hand and pulled one out. He pulled out a lighter, lit it, and toked it. His mind was clouded with thoughts of rage and he was suddenly startled by a knock at his front door. With a mean, loud voice he asked "**WHO THE FUCK IS IT**?!" as he got up and approached the door.

"It's me, Michelle."

He aggressively opened the door with a snarl on his face.

"Oh, wdup? I forgot you were coming by." Demarco said as he unlocked the screen, opened it and walked back into the living room and sat back down on the couch.

Michelle stepped in, holding a brown paper bag in one hand and shut the door behind her with the other. With a funky look on her face she walked over and sat down on the couch and put the bag down on the floor by her feet.

"Damn nigga what the fuck wrong with you?" Michelle asked as she looked over at him.

Demarco just sat there for a couple of seconds staring off into the dining room and replied "Shit; I'm good... What you got in the bag?"

Men-Tal

"See that's why I know it's something wrong with yo ass because you asked me to stop and get some Ciroc on my way over here." Michelle answered with a nigga you trippin type of look on her face.

"Oh yeah my bad, I forgot." Demarco said as he sat up, took a deep breath and rubbed his forehead wanting to get his mind off that bullshit between him and Cognac.

Michelle reached in the bag and pulled out the pint of Ciroc, handed it to him and told him "I know you going through some shit and we gone get yo mind right. However I'm still a lady so that means you gotta open it and pour my drink." Michelle said as she handed him the bottle.

"You right baby, I got you." Demarco replied as he took the bottle.

Demarco tilted the bottle to the side and smacked it on the ass like the fellas do. He then tilted the head of the bottle towards Michelle so that she could stroke the spout of it as if it were the shaft of a dick. Michelle tried to smack the ass of the bottle like Demarco did, but he told her she was doing it wrong. Michelle, confused looked at him and asked "Okay...what am I supposed to do?"

"You gotta stroke the neck and head of the bottle." Demarco answered.

"What?" Michelle asked with a puzzled look on her face.

"You gotta stroke the neck and the head of it. The man smacks the ass of the bottle and the woman strokes the neck and head of the bottle. You know, like a dick, duh. Stop being such a lame." Demarco replied.

"Yall niggas include sex in every fucking thing y'all do. I bet you smack the ass of the Captain Crunch box when you pour your cereal, don't you?" Michelle said sarcastically.

Michelle wrapped her hand around the neck of the bottle and stroked it up and down a couple of times. Demarco twisted the cap off of the bottle and then remembered he needed cups. He looked up and Michelle was already on point holding up two large red plastic cups with the white rim. She sat the cups on the coffee table in front of them then he poured drinks. He looked up and Michelle was on point again holding in her hands a small fifty cent bag of ice cubes and a bottle of Cranberry juice. He took the ice and juice and added it to the drink just right. He looked up and saw that Michelle was on point again, holding up a silver and green packet of weed wraps and a fat twenty sack. Demarco just looked at her for a second, thinking to himself how he really needed this shit to relax his mind. He really just wanted to get his mind on to something else other than the thought of him getting played by Cognac like he wasn't shit.

"Damn, you know you be looking out. You the truth, babe." Demarco said as he handed her, her drink.

"Come on, I got you. Now you want to tell me what's wrong with you? Just don't tell me one of these brauds you been fucking done gave you the HeBeGeBies." Michelle said as she took a swig.

Demarco took a big chug and replied "Naw, I aint got no disease or nothing like that."

He sat there, scoffed at his thoughts and took another swallow.

"Oh, some braud done pussy whipped yo ass and now she aint acting right, huh?" Michelle asked, trying to guess what's wrong with him.

"Hell nall, aint no braud got me pussy whipped!...The bitch, just pissed me off, and now I wanna fuck her ass up." Demarco replied with an ill scowl on his face, and swigged his drink, staring into the dining room.

"Calm down, she aint even worth it. I mean, I know these brauds be making yall wanna beat they ass, but it aint worth y'all going to jail for." Michelle stated.

"Whatever, if I feel like you saying fuck me after I done invested my money into you, it's gone be some severe repercussions coming to you. I don't give a fuck if it's business, bitches, or niggas! Don't fuckin play me." Demarco retorted emphatically.

"SOME BRAUD DONE JACKED YOU FOR YO MONEY?!" Michelle asked with her eyes bucked as she passed him the weed and the papers.

"Hell nall, I aint slippin like that. What it is, I've been dating this chick since the beginning of the year, going out to different places blowing money. Taking her around my peeps, buying her shit, fucking each other all the time; you know we was doing that shit that couples do. And on some real shit, I started loving her ass, but lately she been playing me. She don't answer my calls or return my calls like she normally do, and now I remember why I said I'll never give a bitch my heart. Bitches want to be heartless with the way they do shit, and that's why Ima dog they asses from now on." Demarco impressed as he poured him some more to drink.

"Come on Marco; don't let one chick blow it for the rest of us. Get over that bitch." Michelle said as she bottoms up'ed her cup, finishing her drink and handed him her cup for some more.

"Man, all these brauds say that same shit, and turn around and fuck over you the same way. As a matter of fact she said that bullshit to me, so fuck that shit, and these bitches. From now on I'm dogging em." Demarco replied, as he rolled up a thick joint.

"Let me ask you this. Do you think she's fucking with somebody else? Do this chick got a job or is she a sack chaser?" Michelle asked.

"To be honest with you, I don't know if she fucking with another nigga or what. And as far as work goes, she's a hairstylist over at that um, um Essential Beauty Salon." Demarco answered.

"Essential Beauty Salon? That's where I get my nails and shit did. Matter of fact I was just there the other day. Which one of them hoes, I mean brauds you fucking with up there?" Michelle asked, trying to cover up her natural dislike and envy towards women.

Demarco grabbed his lighter off of the table, and put the joint in his mouth. He sparked the flame at the tip; you could hear the crackle of the weed as he toked. He held it for a nice moment, slowly exhaled and then calmly replied..."Her name is Rachelle, but she go by the name Cognac or Coney."

"You fucking with that bitch, nigga?!" Michelle asked with a real nasty look on her face.

Demarco was caught off guard by her remark and how she said it with such an attitude. He leaned back with a weird look on his face, thinking to himself where did that shit come from.

"Damn, why you say it like that?" Demarco asked as he passed her the blunt.

Michelle took the blunt and toked it. She held it for a moment and exhaled a stream of smoke. She thumped the ashes into the ash tray and replied. "You might not like what I got to say but Ima keep it real with you. Yeah, she playing you." Michelle passed him the blunt.

Demarco looked at her with a straight face "How you know we even talking about the same person?"

"Okay let's see, she's about five-five, five-six, brown skinned. Her hairstyle is long and she built pretty nice." Michelle asked, trying not to make it sound too good.

"Did she have thick hips and a big ass?" Demarco asked.

"Yes nigga, she do. I just aint trying to talk about her body like that." Michelle expressed.

"Okay let's say we are talking about the same person. How you know she playing me?" Demarco asked as he hit the blunt.

"Because she had this one dude come up there and pick her up." She answered.

Immediately he thought back on the night at the New Years Eve Ball when he got into it with Keith. He remembered the dirty looks and all the tuff talk that was coming out of his mouth. It basically renewed his anger and gave him a reason to bring the pain to Keith...even if it cost Cognac her life.

"What the nigga look like?" Demarco asked as he sipped some more of his drink.

"Um, he was tall, bout your height. He had a very low hair-cut, goatee, built very nice and drove a black Charger." Michelle answered.

"Yeah, I know that nigga. I was about to fuck his ass up the night of the New Years Eve Ball for being disrespectful." Demarco expressed emphatically.

"For real, what happened?!" Michelle asked.

"His ass walked up and tried to holla at Cognac while I was standing there talking to her. And when I checked his ass he started running his muthafuckin mouth. I swear on everything, if the police wasn't thick as fuck outside after we left out of there I was gone merk that nigga." Demarco expressed as his nostrils flared and his lips and mouth tightened.

Long time ago Michelle's man tried to holla at Cognac on the sly at a hair show and Michelle despised Cognac ever since. She felt like Cognac had one up on her and could hold that shit over her head if she wanted to. Michelle would love to be able to get at Cognac in any way she could and even the playing field. Michelle's devious mind was thinking of ways to mess up anything for her. Plan A, take Demarco's focus off of Cognac; a petty plan but she really didn't give a damn.

"Look nigga, I came over here to get your mind right. I don't want you trippin over these bitch's, fuck them." Michelle said as she scooted a little closer to him.

"Man fuck that! That bitch been playing me after all I've been doing for her? AND IT'S WITH THAT NIGGA?! Both them muthafucka's can get it." Demarco impressed.

"Marco, stop trippin over they asses right now." Michelle said as she eased her hand on his leg, gradually moving it upward.

Demarco was pissed but couldn't help the fact that Michelle's hand on his leg felt good. He was surprised because Michelle had never come on him like this before. She started rubbing his dick then unzipped his pants. She reached in his pants and pulled out his dick. She leaned over and circulated her tongue around the head of his dick then sucked it. She took it out of her mouth, spit on it and started jacking him off as she tongue bathed his balls. Demarco was in paradise and loving every second of it. She stuck his dick back in her mouth and started sucking it as saliva seeped from her mouth down his shaft and scrotum. She was determined to be his nasty little freak and take a face full of cum shots when it was time for him to blast off. Demarco toked the blunt and gently stroked his fingers through her hair as he palmed her head. He laid his head back on the couch and enjoyed the fuck out of some bomb as head.

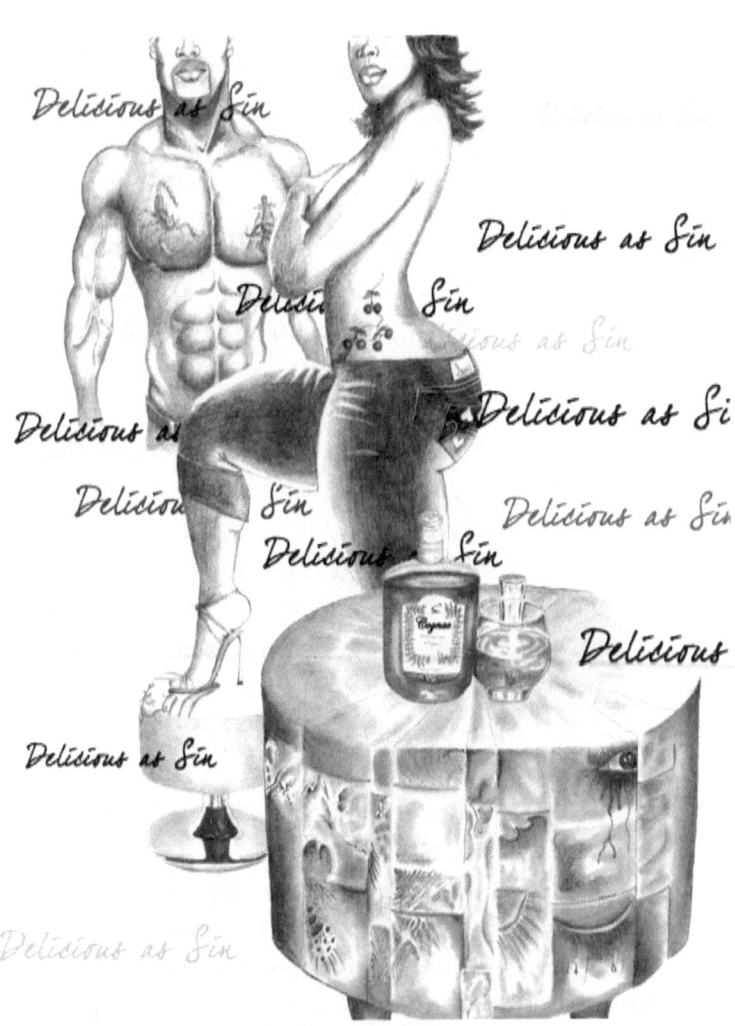

Delicious as Sin

Delicious as Sin

There's nothing in the world more mouth watering than a woman with a nice round ass in some nice fitting jeans and sexy high heels. I mean jeans that ride her hips and curves to perfection, and high heels that raise that ass up and make you want to touch it...make you want to stick your nose all up in it and smell it...make you want to lick and tongue bathe everything she got going on inside them jeans. This is what Keith was thinking as he sat in the chair in his room and admired Cognac's delectable figure as she stood in front of him with her ass facing him. She pulled some items out of a bag and placed them on Keith's bed; a can of whip cream, and a bottle of chocolate syrup. Keith stood up and walked up behind her. He placed passionate wet kisses on her neck as his hands traced and caressed her curvaceous hips. She felt the bulge of his dick poking her ass. She tilted her head as passionate sensations made her nipples erect. His right hand gently caressed her stomach then moved down in between her legs. He stroked her pussy in a circular motion; he could feel the moisture through her pants. She looked back and they started kissing while reaching behind her rubbing his head with her fingernails. Her breathing accelerated as she unbuttoned her shirt, and he unbuttoned her pants. She took off her shirt and tossed it over on the dresser. Her ass seemed to burst out of her jeans as he peeled them down her hips and thighs. He took them off of her, tossing them to the side and made her spread her legs and bend over. Down on his knees, he gripped her ass cheeks, and spread them. Her scent was so fucking arousing to him as he stuck his face all up in that ass and started licking and sucking her pussy from the back. He made her climb up on the edge of the bed in a doggy-style position and then he grabbed the whip cream. He squirted out a thick line of it from her ass down to her pussy and licked off every trace. He squirted more on her pussy and sensually sucked every bit of whipped cream and pussy juice he could possibly ingest. Cognac tightly gripped the bed sheets as the sensation made her just want to explode and cum all on his fucking face. She moaned as her fingertips and toes stiffened. He slowly stood up kissing her all over her ass, all up her back and passionately started kissing the other side of her neck as he caressed her breast with his hands. Cognac grabbed the chocolate syrup then turned around and grabbed his rock hard dick. She squeezed and zigzagged chocolate all down the head and shaft and then bent over and started sucking it. She made him sit back down in the chair behind him as she kneeled down on the floor while keeping her mouth glued to his dick every step of the way. She loved him palming her head as she slid her lips up and down his shaft vertically. She squeezed more chocolate on him and slurped all of it as she gagged and sucked, twirled her tongue around the head, spit on it and started sucking it like her life depended on it... Basically, she sucked the fuck out that nigga dick. He made her get up and get back on the edge of the bed, doggy-style. Her ass never looked rounder and juicier. He stuck his dick in her pussy slow and deep and started fucking her good. He gripped her slim waist and admired as he watched his dick penetrate her thick bulging ass cheeks. He turned her over on her back, and placed her legs around his neck with her booty hanging vulnerably off the edge of the bed. He stuck his dick in and watched in the mirror as he fucked the shit out of her. Cognac felt so fucking good. The feeling was extremely intensified every time his nuts slapped her ass as he repeatedly drilled her pussy. She clutched the bed sheets, and moaned as she creamed profusely. He had her lay on her stomach in the bed and he got on top her. He opened her legs and easily slid his dick in. He had her close her legs, causing her booty and pussy to simultaneously squeeze his dick for the ultimate sensation. His muscles tightened and body stiffened as he got in as many strokes as he could. The feeling became too intense to hold back as he pulled out and jacked his dick, showering her ass with an overload of cum. He turned over on his back and lied there catching his breath. Cognac grabbed his dick and calmly stroked the rest of the cum out.

"Un un baby, don't be getting too comfortable. You got to go get me a towel so I can wipe all this cum off of my ass." Cognac said as she looked back at her ass then at Keith.

"Aw baby just rub it in; you know it's good for the skin. It will have you glowing." Keith replied being funny.

"What, boy go get me a towel, thank you." Cognac said as she laid there feeling good.

Keith got up and went to go get her a towel. She heard the faint sound of her cell phone vibrating in her purse which was on the night table next to the bed. She leaned over and reached in her purse and grabbed it to see who was calling. She didn't get it in time and looked at the screen and saw that she had eight missed calls and six new text messages. She clicked on the missed calls and saw that Demarco had been blowing her phone up with calls. She put her phone back in her purse and laid there. Keith returned with the towel and Cognac sarcastically said "Bout time."

"Whatever, shut up." Keith said as he walked along side of the bed and enjoyed wiping her ass for her.

Keith wiped her clean and dry and then heard his cell phone ring. He walked over to his pants on the floor and grabbed his phone out the belt holster. He saw that it was the furniture company ready to deliver and install his new washer and dryer. He answered the phone and told them that he had forgot that they were coming but everything was all good just give him a minute and he'll be out there to let them in.

"That was the appliance story delivery people telling me they were outside ready to bring in the washer and dryer. I forgot they asses was coming; I still gotta go pick up my clothes from the cleaners before they close, AND WE STILL gotta make that run too." Keith said as he started putting on his gear.

"Baby, you want me to go pick up your clothes for you so that part will be out of the way?" Cognac asked.

"Hell yeah, thank you baby." Keith answered and gave her a kiss on the lips.

Cognac went into the bathroom to briefly wash up.

"Hey, now that was some good birthday sex right there." Cognac said from the bathroom.

"Well that was just the prelude for what's to cum later. Ima have to put a thrashing on that ass before the night is over with." Keith said as he put on his shirt.

"Boy whatever, that's only if you can handle anymore of this ass." Cognac said while washing up.

"Handle? I'm the king of handling shit. Matter of fact I'm the Lebron James of handling that ass. Better yet just call me the MVP of that ass." Keith expressed as he walked over and stood by the bathroom talking shit.

"More like the MVP of bumping them jibs. But since you like talking shit, how about I just sit on your mouth and give you something productive to do with it?" Cognac replied sarcastically.

Keith just stood there for a second and then replied "Damn, that don't sound too bad, but in the mean time go get Big Daddy clothes and we'll pick up on this stuff later."

"You better shut up before you be going to get your own shit." Cognac retorted, playfully.

"HEY, Big Daddy need you to stop running that mouth, and go handle that. I'm about to go downstairs and let these people in." Keith replied as he walked downstairs.

Cognac smiled and shook her head as she dried herself off. She thought about how much fun she has with Keith despite his dangerous lifestyle. She was hoping that he would take his money and invest it in a business that was legitimate. I guess you can say she was dangerously in love with playing with fire. She put on her clothes and walked down the stairs, and into the kitchen.

"Keith, where the keys at babe?" Cognac asked.

Keith was looking out of the living room window at the delivery men seeing if they were walking up yet. He walked into the kitchen with his keys in his hand.

"Here you go." Keith said as he handed her the keys then hurried up and snatched them back before she could get a good grip on them.

"What?" Cognac asked, responding to him snatching back the keys.

"Now you take care of my baby." Keith said jokingly referring to his car as he dangled the keys between the tips of his index finger and thumb.

"Boy bye! Give me them damn keys. Ima teach you how to ride that thang the right way." Cognac said, playfully snatching them from him.

Keith shook his head and just looked at her sexy ass as she walked to the door.

"Don't be trying to stunt and get no numbers in my shit." Keith said, humorously, but slightly serious.

Before Cognac could open the door she stopped, took her sunglasses out of her purse and put them in her hair. She glanced back at her ass then looked back at him like whatever nigga. She smirked, blew him a kiss and walked out the door. In the mean time the delivery men were sitting in their truck getting their invoices together till Keith told them to come in. In the process of doing so the driver, Demetrius peeped Cognac walking out the door and started tapping the shit out of his partner's leg trying to get his attention.

"OH MY MUTHAFUCKIN GAUD! Look at this woman's muthafuckin hips. I can look at her from the front and tell she got a big ass booty." Demetrius expressed emphatically.

Patrick, his partner was looking down on the floor in between the two seats trying to find what they did with Keith's invoice. Patrick was kind of blasé towards Demetrius for what he was saying till he looked up and saw for his self.

"Man whatever dog, you said that the last time and braud wasn't about shit." Patrick replied nonchalantly.

"Nigga, look, I aint bullshiting!" Demetrius impressed.

Patrick looked up and to his lustful surprise he said "**GAUD DAMN SHE GOT A FAT ASS!**" Patrick replied excitedly as he was caught off guard with eyes wide as fuck.

"I know my man happily fucking the shit out of that big ass." Demetrius said sincerely.

"Hell yeah, he better be, because I would for damn sho!" Patrick said, eyes transfixed on her figure.

"Man you wouldn't even know what to do with all that ass, nigga." Demetrius said as they watched her get in the car.

"Nigga, you out yo muthafucking mind! I'll spank that ass like African drums at an Ethiopian get-together all damn night. You would think it was war drums being played up in this bitch." Patrick said as they stared at her as she started the car.

Cognac knew they were checking her out, but she never looked there way. She just smirked to herself and slightly shook her head as she rolled down the windows and pulled off.

Can't Keep Running from the Mess You've Made

Two ladies by the name of Deanna and Kenya walked inside of Seven Mile Cleaners just off of Wyoming Street. A guy by the name of Marlon was sweeping the floor as they walked in and approached the counter.

"I'll be with you Goddesses in one second." Marlon said with a smile as he swept the dirt on the floor into the dust pan.

"Goddesses?" Deanna asked, wondering why he called her that.

The nasty look on her face showed that she really wasn't digging his respectable acknowledgment. She was used to hoodlums and thugs and had no respect for a respectable and honorable Black Man...A King. Marlon looked over at her and said "Yes, I called you a Goddess, my sista. That's honor."

"Oh yeah, well...whatever." Deanna uttered to Kenya.

"I apologize if I am taking too long." Marlon said.

"Oh, don't rush on the count of me. It's okay, sir, take your time." Deanna said as she briefly glanced at him with a whatever nigga type of look on her face.

Kenya was reading Deanna's mind as they looked at each other and chuckled to themselves. Marlon dumped the dirt into a garbage bag and twisted it up and then took it behind the counter and shut the door. He approached the counter and greeted them respectfully.

"Hey, how may I help you ladies today?" Marlon asked with a smile.

"Yeah, I'm here to pick up my clothes." Deanna said and handed him her order ticket.

He glanced at it and said "I'll be right back."

As he walked away to go get her order Deanna just looked at him with a real stank ass look on her face.

"Damn D, why you look at ole boy like that?" Kenya asked as she glanced at Marlon then back at Deanna.

"Because, I can't stand niggas that come at you all deep and shit. I mean, I don't like all that whack ass hello Goddess bullshit. I need a real nigga to talk to me." Deanna answered.

"Don't talk about your baby daddy like that. He aint ugly." Kenya said being funny and laughing.

"Whatever! I don't care how cute a nigga is. I wish the fuck I would holla a nigga that sweep floors at a fucking cleaners. That's like going on a date with a nigga that work at Top Hat, Jeepers or Chucky Cheeses or something. I mean, he can only afford to take you to the Dollar Show and that's only if his car can make it there." Deanna said.

"Girl you is stupid." Kenya replied as she laughed her ass off.

"Whatever, I'm for real. I need me a baller, a nigga that got that bread. A nigga who can take me places and buy me nice things. Matter of fact; what he can do is introduce me to the owner of this muthafucka, now that's who I'll holla at." Deanna said, tooting her lips.

"Girl, yes I feel you. I aint got time to be kicking it with no broke ass nigga." Kenya replied.

They quieted down and changed the subject as he came back to the window with her items.

"Here you are Ms. Deanna, that will be seventeen-fifty." Marlon said as he put the clothes through the fiberglass door.

Deanna reached down in her purse and took out a wrinkled up twenty dollar bill, and handed it to him. He rung the total up in the cash register and then gave her the change.

"Thank you." Deanna said real dry as she grabbed her clothes and they turned and headed for the door.

"Hey, excuse me. I want to give y'all a couple of flyers to a show of poetry, singing, and live music I'm performing in next Wednesday." Marlon said, stopping them in their tracks as they turned around.

"No, not interested." Deanna answered nonchalantly.

"No, I'm straight." Kenya replied as well.

As they walked out they bumped into Cognac as she was walking up to the door.

"Wsup Coney, Happy Birthday." Deanna said as she gave her a hug.

"Thank you D. I think we are supposed to be hanging out at the club later on tonight. You should come and get your party on." Cognac said.

"Yeah, I'm definitely with that. Oh, this is my girl Kenya. Kenya this is a friend of mine, Cognac." Deanna said, introducing them.

"Nice to meet you." Cognac said with a smile as she shook her hand.

"Nice to meet you." Kenya replied.

"Well, we are about to get on out of here; got some runs to make. We will just catch up with you later." Deanna said.

"Okay, see y'all then." Cognac replied as she proceeded to walk into the cleaners.

A few seconds after walking away Deanna said "That bitch swear she the shit. I look way better than her."

Inside Cognac approached the counter with Keith's order ticket in hand. Marlon found her very attractive as she walked in, and played it cool as she approached the counter.

"Good afternoon. How may I help you?" Marlon asked with a smile.

"Yes, I'm here to pick up some clothes for Keith Richmond." Cognac answered, handing him the order ticket.

"Okay I'll be right back." Marlon said as he went back to get the clothes.

As Cognac patiently waited for Marlon to bring her the clothes she pondered the direction she was headed in her life. How she wasn't getting any younger and eventually wanted to be someone's wife. But before she could achieve such a beautiful reality she had to first look within. She had to realize the changes that she needed to work on;

mentally, spiritually, and emotionally and sever the bitterness from her past relationship and move forward. By then Marlon was on his way back to the counter with the clothes. He hung them on a near by clothes rack. He grabbed her ticket and rung up her total.

"Thirty-seven fifty." Marlon said, thinking to himself how appealing she was to him.

"Okay." Cognac responded then reached in her purse and took out the money and handed it to him.

Marlon cashed her out and then passed her the clothes through the fiberglass doors. He wanted to try and get her telephone number but then he figured maybe she was there to pick up the clothes for her man. But then he thought that maybe it could've been her brother, father, or cousin that she was picking up clothes for so why not at least ask her if she had a man. Just as Cognac was about to turn around and leave Marlon got her attention.

"Excuse me." Marlon said with a charming smile...

"Hey." Cognac replied as she looked at him.

"I just wanted to ask you if you had a man, sweetie." Marlon asked.

"Yes, I have someone I'm seeing right now." Cognac replied.

"So he aint your man, he's just someone you're getting to know?" Marlon asked.

"Yes." Cognac replied.

"I respect that. He is a blessed man to have a beautiful, and honorable woman such as yourself. I pray that I can find a Goddess like you." Marlon said with a smile.

Cognac smiled because that compliment made her feel very nice.

"Goddess, huh? Thank you." Cognac replied with a smile as she turned and walked away.

"Have a blessed day." Marlon said as he admired her figure as she walked away.

"Okay, thank you. You have a blessed day too." Cognac looked back and said as she walked out holding the clothes by the hanger over her shoulder.

Cognac remotely unlocked the car as she approached it. She opened the back door on the driver's side and hung his clothes up on the clothes hook right by the window. She shut the back door and then opened the front door. Her cell phone started vibrating as she got in the driver's seat, shutting the door behind her. She had been getting Happy Birth Day text messages all day. She picked up her phone and started replying to Regina's text. As she was typing on her touch screen Demarco just happened to call at the time and she made a mistake and touched the answer icon. "Fuck!" She silently uttered to herself as she looked at her phone.

"Hello?" Demarco said, wondering why she didn't say anything when she answered.

Cognac did not feel like talking to him right then and reluctantly responded "Hey Demarco."

"I don't want to take up to much of your time; I know you a busy woman and things. So I just want to say Happy Birthday, and I wish you many more." Demarco said, unable to hide that he was pissed.

"Oh, thank you Demarco. Maybe we can go out or something." Cognac said as she started the car.

"Oh, you want to go out? Oh okay, I guess we can throw that in the schedule at some point of time. I know you real busy now days, but what you can do is come by real quick and pick up this gift I bought you." Demarco suggested.

Cognac did not want to go over there, especially not right then. She knew that she had been blowing Demarco off and was feeling a little guilty for doing so. She took a deep breath and asked "Um...right now?"

"Yeah, because I got a lot of stuff to do and I don't know when Ima be able to holla at you." Demarco replied.

"You can't give it to me later?" Cognac asked as she pulled off.

"Damn, you playing me like that now? I done spent all this money on you and you just can't slide by and pick your gift up? I aint trying to hold you up from doing nothing you trying to do; you aint even gotta come in if you don't want to. I just want you to come get your gift and you can go." Demarco said.

"Damn, why you gotta say it so cold sounding?" Cognac asked.

"I aint trying to sound cold, but you the one who's been treating a nigga all cold. We was spending time, going out doing shit, chillin, blowin money, fucking each other, and then all of a sudden my money, energy and time aint valued no more." Demarco stressed, sounding pissed.

"It aint like that, Demarco." Cognac replied, feeling slightly pressured.

"Well then why don't you just come by and get the gift that I bought you and you can finish handling your business?" Demarco suggested.

Cognac felt pressured and pressed for time because she didn't want to be gone with Keith's car for too long. She figured she could shoot by, say what's up, get her birthday gift and leave right out being that he already knew she was doing something.

"Okay, I'll come over real quick. I just didn't want to come over and leave right out like that but I'm on my way." Cognac answered.

"Alright, see you when you get here." Demarco said and hung up.

Numerous thoughts about her situation with Keith and Demarco were running through her mind as she listened to the radio and drove through traffic. The deep love song seemed to go right along with her thoughts. She knew deep down inside that she was going to have to end it with Demarco. She understood that both of them had feelings for her but she decided she wanted to focus on her and Keith. And then she remembered the knowledgeable words of her cousin Regina... "You can crap out, but you can't live twice."

After ten or fifteen minutes of driving she finally arrived at his street and made a right. She cruised to the middle of the block and pulled over in front of his house. Demarco noticed the black Charger as she pulled up and was looking like what the fuck. He thought to himself that she had a lot of muthafucking nerve to come to his house in Keith's car. This bitch must have a death wish, he said out loud as he got up and walked to the door. She got out of the car and locked it. About eight or nine guys were all on the porch next door gawking at her and making comments as she walked up on Demarco's porch. A couple of dudes who were sitting in a car parked across the street, adjacent from Demarco's house. They stopped their conversation and lustfully made comments about her as well. She got ready to ring the door bell and the door suddenly opened partially. She stood there for a second thinking he was going to open the door for her all the way, but...he didn't. She opened the door for herself thinking he must be mad still. She walked in and he was sitting down on the couch looking out the window as if she wasn't there. Her mind state was to keep it very brief and get the hell up out of there.

"Um...hello Demarco." Cognac said with an eyebrow raised and feeling a little awkward.

"Your gift in there on the dining room table." Demarco responded, still looking outside.

Cognac just looked at him for a second, shook her head and walked in the dining room. She noticed a rectangular box on the table with her name on it and picked it up. She took the lid off and saw a platinum necklace with a charm that read "SEXY". She loved it and her guilty feeling had just gotten heavier. She turned around and speechlessly looked at him as he was getting up off the couch and walking over to her.

"You like it?" Demarco asked.

"I love it, it's beautiful. Demarco you didn't have to buy this." Cognac replied, not wanting to look at him in his eyes as guilt was convicting her.

"I know I didn't, but it's a token of how I feel about you." Demarco replied as he took the necklace and gently fastened it around her neck.

"Yes, but I can't take this." Cognac said.

"Girl, you better take this. I aint taking no for an answer now put it on." Demarco said, looking her firmly in the eyes.

Cognac took a deep breath and replied "Alright."

"Well, I know you gotta go, I aint gone hold you up like I said I wouldn't. Just call me if you get a chance." Demarco said, wanting her to leave.

"Okay, Ima call you later." Cognac said as she kissed him on the jaw and made her way to the door.

"Oh, and Happy Birthday." Demarco said.

"Thank you, Demarco." Cognac said as she opened the door and stepped out on the porch.

Demarco smirked; thinking to himself she really think shit is all good and said "Okay, you're welcome. You be safe and enjoy your birthday."

Cognac turned and walked off the porch and headed to the car. The dudes on the porch next door made more comments on her shape and talking about how lucky Demarco was. Demarco picked up his cell phone and dialed a number as he watched through the window as she got in the car. The driver who was sitting across the street in the car picked up his phone and answered.

"Wuz good?" Wayne answered as he sat there staring down at his pistol in his hand.

"Don't knock her off just yet, stick to the plan. And it just got that much easier because she's driving that nigga car so she gone lead you right to his ass. I want you to follow that bitch and do them both at the same time. We kill two birds with one shot. You feel me? And tell that nigga Loose-Screws I said don't lose my fucking gun doing no wild dumb shit. Tell him I said bring it back to me in the same way I let him see it." Demarco said, thinking to himself he should've never let Loose-Screws use his gun.

"Not a problem playboy, I got you." Wayne said as he hung up, started his car, put on his shades, turned it around and followed her.

"Hell yeah, I'm ready to blast a muthafucka right about now." Loose screws said from the passenger seat and put on his shades as well.

Wayne carefully mimicked every move she made as she drove through Seven Mile Rd's crazy traffic. He didn't get to close up on her though so she wouldn't recognize him.

Cognac was on the phone with Keith telling him that she was about to pull up so he could come on outside so they could go. She arrived at Plainview Street and made a right turn. A group of females were outside arguing about to fight each other five on five. Cognac was looking like what the fuck as she maneuvered her way through them seconds before they got to scrapping. Wayne had to slam on brakes as all ten women were fighting from the side walk to the streets. They cussed, threw wild punches, scratched and slammed each other up against cars in the middle of street. A couple ladies had their shirts ripped off as tits flopped everywhere. Children were outside screaming and crying as they witnessed the ladies violently trying to beat the shit out of each other. Family members ran out in the street trying to break up the troubling scene. Wayne saw Keith come out of the house and get in the car as he and Cognac pulled off. Wayne blew his horn quite hostile trying to get the wild fighting ass women to get the hell out of the way. They kept fighting and could give a fuck less about him blowing his horn. Loose Screws was a hostile blast first type of dude who didn't give a fuck about putting a bullet in a woman as easy as he would a dude. He put his pistol out the window of the car and shot off five loud ass rounds in the air and yelled "Get the fuck out the muthafuckin way!!!" People scurried for their lives as they screamed in terror while looking for the children, screaming run and get down! Wayne sped through, just inches away from running over one lady who was trying to get up off of the ground, barely making it out of the way. He ignorantly drove top speed up the block endangering the lives of children who were outside playing like kids should and enjoying life. He immediately slammed on brakes as he got to the corner, skidding pass the stop sign. Pedestrians crossing the street had to jump back or hurry across to avoid getting killed. They looked both ways trying to see which way Cognac and Keith went. They skidded off towards the right in pursuit to find them. After five minutes of searching they had given up on trying to finding them. Wayne took his phone out and called Demarco.

"Tell me something good." Demarco said, expecting good news.

"I aint even about to talk you to death with no bullshit. We was trailing ole girl perfectly. Then right when we got ready to turn the corner behind her about a hundred brauds ran into the street and started fighting. By time we made they asses get the fuck out the way old girl and ya man's had pulled off and we couldn't find they ass. But trust me my nigga, I promise you I got you." Wayne stressed.

"Come on my nigga, you can't be out there slippin like that dog. I need you to handle that shit."

"I know, don't even sweat it big dog. I'ma ride down on their ass before the night is over with, I put that on everything I love." Wayne impressed sincerely.

Demarco got off of the phone with Wayne, exhaled and rubbed his face, feeling frustration. He walked into the kitchen and grabbed a beer out of the refrigerator then turned around and leaned up against the counter. He twisted the cap off and took a huge guzzle. His cell phone chimed, alerting him that he had just received a text message. It was from a chick named Jasmine who he had done some party promotions with in the past. Jasmine was also a very good friend with Cognac and all three of them knew it. Jasmine sent out a text message to everyone in her phone who she thought was affiliated and cool with Cognac. It was a text promoting Cognac's birthday party at Aunt Val's house with the street, address, and time. Demarco stood there in amazement with a slight smirk on his face. Then with squinted eyes he nodded his head and sinisterly said to himself in a very slow fashion "Thank you, Jasmine... You just made shit a whole lot easier."

SURPRISE!!!!

9:37pm Keith and Cognac had been cruising the streets all day, having fun for her birthday. He took her to Macy's and bought her a couple of designer purses, and two pairs of the hottest Stiletto's on the shelves. He also bought her a couple of Baby Phat jeans and tops top's to match. They had been downtown by Hart Plaza enjoying the atmosphere. They had also rode up the famous Jefferson street going eastward and circled around Belle Isle a couple of times, getting their sip on. Ice cubes swirled in their plastic red cups as Cognac poured them some more Hennessey, chased with a little cola. It's something about the beautiful city night life. Multiple streetlights, nice music and a little liquor constitutes a feeling so surreal. They were going to end the night off by hanging out at Club Elise with Regina, Benita and some other friends. Cognac text Regina, and let her know that they were on their way over to her house. Regina had asked her to pick up her purse from over Aunt Valerie's house because she made a mistake and left it over there earlier. About seven or eight minutes later they had arrived at Aunt Val's house. She remembered that Aunt Val had told her that she and her son, Eric were going over to Uncle Gary's house to visit and perhaps would spend the night. Cognac told Keith that he could come in and use the restroom if he needed to.

"Why does my Auntie leave every light off every time she leaves out, knowing it will be dark before she gets back?" Cognac asked as they got out of the car.

"I don't know but I gotta piss like a fucking race horse, I'll tell you that much." Keith replied as he shut the car door behind him.

"Me to, for real. It feels like I've been holding it since yesterday." Cognac replied.

"Damn, I love the way your ass move when you walk." Keith said as he watched her walk up on the porch.

"Keep your eyes off my booty." Cognac said as she put her hand behind her ass as if she could really cover it up.

"In other words you want me to keep looking at it. That's why you said it like that." Keith said, dexterously smirking as he licked his lips.

Cognac stuck her key in the door lock, but before she turned the key to unlock it she turned around. With both her index fingers she grabbed him by his belt loops on his pants and pulled him close to her. She looked at him in his eyes and sincerely said "Yes, I love you admiring my body, it makes me feel very good. I love our sex life, I love the way you touch me, and hold me. But more importantly I need to know that you're paying attention to my mind and what I stand for morally as well."

"Baby, trust me I do. I think you are a very intelligent woman, and you carry yourself like one at all times. I wouldn't respect you the way I do if I didn't respect your mind. But also understand that your intelligence and beauty together is an aphrodisiac." Keith said sincerely.

Cognac just looked at him for a second with a slight smirk on her face.

"Mmm, mmm, mmm boy, you are good with them words. You know just what to say to make me feel super good." Cognac said, shaking her head in amazement.

"Seriously I mean it. And you know what else? I've been really thinking about us. I really want us to be an official couple. You know, I'm for real, and I'm still standing by every promise I made when we were at the **Bistro**." Keith stressed.

Cognac took a deep breath and looked at him with a straight face.

"Keith, I've been thinking about us to, and everything you promised as well. I would love to be in an exclusive relationship with you. But Keith, your street life makes all that official couple stuff hard to look forward to. I don't want to live my life constantly looking over my shoulder hoping that don't nothing bad happen to you, me or my son." Cognac said as she looked away.

"Baby, don't look away, I don't want you to lose faith in me. I know it aint no positive future out here in these streets and I got to let it go... Look I promised you Ima let it go and Ima stick to that promise. I just need to get the rest of my paper off these streets and I'm out the game." Keith said as he caressed the side of her face with his hand.

Cognac looked at him with all hope in her eyes and replied "I hope you really mean that, Keith."

"I do baby." Keith said as they hugged each other.

They French kissed for a couple of minutes as their hands roamed and touched each other intimately. Reluctantly she pushed back after enjoying a sexually stimulating kiss.

"Look, we better stop before we be fucking in my Aunties house, and that aint a good idea." Cognac said, breathing deeply.

"Yeah, well...this moment will be continued after all the partying is over. You feel me?" Keith asked.

"Not as much as I want to feel you right now. But um, my bladder just reminded me that I gotta go in here and use the bathroom." Cognac said as she turned around unlocking the door with her legs wiggling back and forth, trying to hold her pee.

"Hell yeah, me to." Keith replied.

Cognac opened the door and they stepped in, shutting the door behind them. She reached for the light switch and flipped it on. "SURPRISE!!!!!!!" Everyone yelled as soon as the light popped on. Cognac and Keith were looking more surprised than a lady with big eyes and no eyebrows after being caught off guard.

"Y'all scared the heck out of me!" Cognac said with a smile as she hugged Regina, her son, Eric and everybody who was there.

It was all smiles, laughter, and partying from there on. The DJ put on the music and it was on and poppin. Keith also was all smiles as he spoke to Regina and who was standing right there as soon as they came in the door. Cognac introduced Keith to Aunt Val, her friends and family that had never met him before. Benita walked up loud and silly as she always is.

"Bout time you showed up! I got tired of kneeling down on my knees like I was at the Alter praying." Benita said hilariously.

"Awwww sweetie, you was anxious to see me, boo?" Cognac asked with a joyous smile.

"Hell yeah because Aunt Val said we couldn't eat until you got here, and I'm starving!" Benita replied.

Cognac stood there with her mouth open, and hand on her hip.

"You mean to tell me you just wanted me here so you can get your grub on?" Cognac asked, laughing.

Benita looked to her right and saw someone trying to fix them a plate of food.

"Oh hell nall, we aint supposed to mess with the food just yet." Benita said to the big fella who was standing next to the food with his Styrofoam plate and plastic fork in his hand.

"Don't wait on me, yall go ahead and eat." Cognac said.

"Well in that case I'm first in the food line so look on out, big fella!" Benita said very animated and darted over to the food.

Cognac laughed at Benita and then she and Keith rushed to the restroom. In the meantime Regina walked into the kitchen and grabbed the birthday cake and brought it out and sat it on the table alongside the gifts. Reonna called Regina on the phone to see if Cognac had made it there yet, and if she had missed the surprise. She told her that she had just pulled up out front and to open the door for her. Regina went to the door and opened it. Reonna walked up on the porch and came in holding a colorful bag.

"Hey, girl you look so pretty." Regina said as Reonna locked the screen door behind her.

"Thank you Gina, I'm just trying to keep up with you." Reonna replied as they hugged each other.

"Whaaaaaat, your boo aint come with you?" Regina asked.

"Oh he should be pulling up any moment. He and Marlon had to make a run earlier so I just told them to meet me over here." Reonna replied.

"Well, as you can see the party is already on and poppin." Regina said as they walked into the living room.

"I see. Where Coney at?" Reonna asked, looking around.

"She in there somewhere." Regina answered.

They proceeded into the dining room and ran right into Cognac and Keith as they standing there talking Aunt Valerie.

"There's my beautiful cousin!" Reonna said, walking up to her with her arms open.

"Wsup, boo?!" Cognac replied in a high pitch voice as they hugged each other.

"You, birthday girl." Reonna answered, handing Cognac the colorful bag she came in with.

"Aw thank you cuz." Cognac said with a smile as she opened the bag.

Cognac looked in the bag and pulled out of bottle of ED Harding perfume for women, and placed it back in the bag. Then she reached inside again and pulled out a fifth of Patron.

"You trying to get your girl blowed, huh?" Cognac asked as she hugged her.

"Hey aint nothing wrong with getting your blow on, I mean ya drink on. Sorry Auntie." Reonna said, laughing.

"We know where YOUR mind is at?" Cognac said sarcastically.

"Yeah, in the Gutter." Aunt Val said playfully as they all laughed.

"No It's not Auntie, I'm a good girl. Haven't I always been your little angel since we was little." Reonna said as she kissed Aunt Valerie on the cheek and looked at her with the innocent face.

"Yeah, when you were little. But now you've grown.....horns." Aunt Valerie said, on a role with her sarcasm.

"Eewwww Auntie, how you gone talk about your little angel like that?" Reonna asked, playfully making a sad face.

"You know you will always be my little angel. Matter of fact both of y'all are my angels." Aunt Valerie said making Reonna and Cognac smile, feeling like little girls inside.

Men-Tal

Eric was in the den playing his Xbox 360 with his cousins and friends. He came out the room and called Aunt Valerie because one of the kids had lost their turn and didn't want to give up the joystick. So she excused herself and went to the den to address them.

"Reonna, I'm sorry for being rude. This is my friend, Keith. Keith, this is my cousin Reonna." Cognac said, introducing them as they greeted each other and shook hands.

"So, are we still hanging out at the club after this, or was that just a ploy for the surprise party?" Reonna asked.

"I guess so. Ima go holla at Regina, and everybody and see if they're game to go to the club." Cognac said.

"Okay, well while you're doing that Ima go over here and speak to Deanna and Kenya since they wanna sit over there all anti-social and not talk to nobody." Reonna said as she walked over to them, messing with them for being so anti.

Cognac and Keith went on enjoying the party talking and laughing with everybody.

There was a knock at the door and Regina heard it then went and answered it. It was Reonna's boyfriend, Charles and his boy,

Marlon. Regina unlocked the door and opened it.

"Wdup Mr. Charles?" Regina asked, greeted him with a smile and a hug.

"Wdup, Gina? I see y'all got it going on over here." Charles said as he looked around.

"Oh most definitely, and we just getting started." Regina replied.

"Oh Gina, this is my boy Marlon. Marlon, this is one of Reonna's cousins, Regina." Marlon said as Regina and Marlon greeted each other.

Regina walked them through kindly introducing them to people who were in the living room. Kenya noticed Marlon as he walked in, looking at him and thinking to herself where does she know him from. With strong curiosity written on her face it all of a sudden hit her that he was the guy from the cleaners. With her eyes focused at Marlon she repeatedly tapped Deanna on the arm trying to get her attention.

"Aw hell nall girl, there go your Baby Daddy." Kenya said humorously interrupting their conversation about men.

"What? Who the hell he know up in here?" Deanna asked with her face frowned up in shitty disgust.

Men-Tal

"That nigga came to find his Baby Momma." Kenya said, laughing.

"Whatever, that broke ass nigga will be wasting his time trying to holla at me." Deanna replied.

"Who y'all talking about?" Reonna asked with an eyebrow raised, thinking to herself they better not be talking about her man.

"Ole boy right there in the black shirt." Deanna answered.

"Who Marlon, y'all know him?" Reonna asked.

"Yeah, that sucka always trying to holla at me every time he see me. I had to diss his lame ass today though." Deanna answered.

"Really? Marlon is a good catch, and he nice looking." Reonna said, shocked that Deanna said that.

"Girl, I aint caught up in that looks shit no more. You got to have some serious cheddar to get with me. I refuse to date a grown ass man that sweeps floors at the damn cleaners. I'm sorry, I can't do it; he aint even on my level." Deanna stressed, shaking her head.

"I'm with you on that shit. Cute looks, and good dick is great but it aint gone pay the bills. Them nigga's can kick rocks with that shit." Kenya concurred, laughing.

"I hear you Deanna, but how you gone demand that a man has to have all these mega bucks when you not even working at all?" Reonna asked.

"Um, when you look this good, and got a body like this you don't have to work. It's a privilege to be with me sweetie. Now what Marlon ass should have done was introduced to the owner of cleaners. You know what I'm saying?" Deanna replied.

"Preach girl!" Kenya said, high fiving Deanna.

Reonna looked at her with a slight smirk on her face and replied "He did introduce you to the owner."

With an incredulous look on Deanna's face she replied "Um, whatever you drinking got you just saying anything now. I never said he introduced me to the owner. I said he needs to introduce me to the owner." Deanna retorted, sarcastically doing the quote unquote signal with her fingers.

"I heard exactly what you said loud and clear, and that's why I said he did introduce you to the owner. He is the owner of that cleaners. Now if y'all two divas will excuse me I have to go fix a plate for my man. Holla at y'all in a minute." Reonna said as she got up and walked into the living room, leaving Deanna and Kenya behind with dumb looks on their faces.

Reonna walked into the living room and hugged her man, and spoke to Marlon. Regina, Cognac, and Keith were laughing at something Regina said as they walked into the living room.

"Is that Charles in the house? Wsup cuz?" Cognac said in an excited high pitch tone of voice.

"Wdup cuz?!" Charles replied as he gave her a hug.

"Wdup doh, big dog?!" Charles asked Keith as he gave him some dap and a hug.

Cognac and Marlon glanced at each other and immediately knew that they knew each other.

"Hey, don't I know you from somewhere?" Marlon asked Cognac.

Cognac briefly felt sort of on the spot as she tried to recall where she remembered him from. It was all eyes on her as she replied "Yeah...you're the guy from the cleaners, right?"

"Yeah, I thought that was you from earlier! Man, it's a small world. How you doing?" Marlon asked as he extended his hand for a handshake.

Cognac knew Keith was definitely paying attention as she answered with a smile and shook his hand "I'm alright, just enjoying my birthday."

"Wow, happy birthday. How old are you?" Marlon asked.

"Hey, hey that's top secret information right there." Cognac replied.

"Well, you look absolutely gorgeous and not a day over twenty-two." Marlon said, making Cognac feel even more on the spot.

"Thank you very much. Hey, let me introduce you to my friend, Keith. Keith, this is Marlon. He rung up the order when I went to go pick up your clothes." Cognac said as she introduced them.

Keith and Marlon shook hands respectfully. In that brief few seconds of respectful smiles and embrace they established very informal eye contact. Marlon knew that Keith could tell that he was very attracted to Cognac and would love to have her under his wing. Keith knew that Marlon could feel his vibe that he was with Cognac and he wasn't playing that disrespect shit or there would be a problem. Those moments are not the most comfortable of times so Regina broke the monotony with the perfect subject, DRINKS.

"Aye, who's going to the store so we can get some more drinks? They done killed them last couple bottles." Regina asked, looking at Cognac hoping she catches on.

Cognac read Regina's mind exactly, and looked up at Keith "Baby, can we go to the store, I need to get something from there anyway?"

"That's cool, let's go." Keith replied, noticing the strange necklace she had on and just curious about whom she had gotten it from or if she had purchased it herself.

As planned the birthday party continued to go great as people ate and enjoyed themselves. Eric came in the front room to ask Cognac if he could have some more of Aunt Valerie's delicious cheesecake. Eric liked Keith so when he saw him he excitedly started talking to him and asking him a bunch of questions. Regina found out who all wanted to chip in on the drink funds so they could go ahead and make the store run. The night was hype, and definitely heating up......

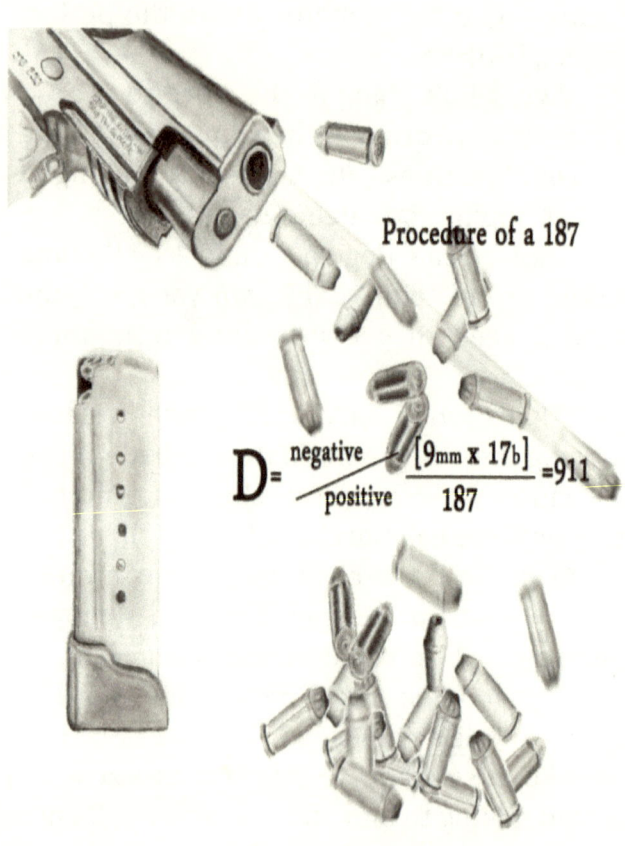

Procedure of a 187

$$D = \frac{\text{negative}}{\text{positive}} \frac{[9_{mm} \times 17_{b}]}{187} = 911$$

Procedure of a 187

Men-Tal

PROCEDURES OF A 187

The corner of Aunt Valerie's Street was dark because the street light had blown out. Wayne and Loose-Screws sat patiently inside of the car just up under it, observing the scene. They were not going to miss this time. Loose-Screws was in the back seat so he could fire out the back window and Wayne could have a clear shot out the front. The sound of metal sliding together was like music to the ears as a clip filled with Black Talon bullets was slipped up inside the gun. Black leather gloves allowed for the perfect grip as Wayne pulled back the slide, cocking the pistol. Wayne's eyes scoped the scene vigilantly and periodically looked back at Loose-Screws through the rearview mirror. In adoration Wayne looked at his gun, slowly rotating it with his hand as he spoke in an ill, poetic manner...

"My nigga... in order to pull off the perfect 187 you must first become one with the gun...this here Colt Forty-Five pistol is my wife, my bitch, my hoe, she's got my back, she keeps me rich...I call her passion because I keep the passion blasting and burning. And these Black Talon bullets are so fucking gorgeous. I love how they rotate as they release from the barrel and explode into razor sharp claws at the tip ripping through the body on impact. And when it penetrates the flesh the claws peel backwards, lacerating and nestling itself in the tissues causing internal damage and bleeding. This here my brother is the art of murder. I get a fuckin hard on just from thinking of this shit." Wayne passionately expressed.

Just as Wayne finished up talking, Loose-Screws looked up and saw Keith and Cognac walking down the driveway from out of the side door as they were on their way to the store to buy more drinks for the party.

"Well guess what my nigga, its show time cause there they asses go right there." Loose-Screws said as he cocked his nickel plated gun.

"Perfect." Wayne said as he started his car and pulled off.

As Cognac, and Keith were just about to cross the street to go get in the car Aunt Val had remembered that she needed something else from the store. She asked little Eric to run and catch them and let them know that she had forgot to ask them to get some toilet paper and paper towel. Eric darted out the door, calling his mother's name but didn't take the money Aunt Valerie had tried to hand to him. Aunt Valerie shook her head, took a deep breath and came out to hand them the money herself. With everything that was happening no one was even paying attention to the car that was approaching. Cognac and Keith had their backs turned towards the street as they were talking to Eric and Aunt Valerie as she was walking up. Too bad they didn't get the memo that death was approaching mercilessly. Wayne and Loose-Screws could give a fuck less about blasting anyone including the elderly and children... their just casualties of street violence. Loose-Screws had a wicked scowl on his face as he raised his pistol. His index finger had about two pounds of pressure on a four pound trigger. With one eye closed, Wayne steady aimed the cross-hair on the gun directly at Cognac's head, slowly pulling the trigger... Immediately the sound of police sirens caught everyone's attention as they put their spotlight on a strange looking man who was at the corner. The man fit the description of someone who had just stolen from a nearby gas station so they stopped him and asked him a few questions. Wayne and Loose-Screws immediately put their guns down. Loose swiftly laid down in the back seat as Wayne calmly cruised past them and turned left at the corner. Though he appeared relaxed his heart pounded as he looked back through the rearview mirror just hoping the police didn't suspect anything strange about them. Everything settled and died down; the police let the guy go on about his business and they slowly cruised up the block. Aunt Valerie and Eric went on back in the house, and Keith and Cognac went and got in the car.

"I see you got yourself an admirer in the house." Keith said as he started the car and eased off.

"What you talking about?" Cognac asked, and giggled.

"Whatever Negro, you know who I'm talking about. Your ass love acting clueless." Keith replied, smiling.

"Me no speak no English, holmes." Cognac said funny and sarcastic as Keith pulled up at the stop sign and kept his foot on the break.

"Well, I hope yo ass understand French because them my Muthafuckin goodies now." Keith said with a smile and squinted eyes.

"Okay, can you translate that for me?" Cognac asked as she sat back, looking at him with an eyebrow raised.

"In other words that's my pussy now." Keith said in a playful manner though he was serious.

"Oh, you running this shit now? It's just official like that, huh?" Cognac asked, blushing.

"Yup." Keith answered as he leaned over and they tongue kissed.

Cognac had gotten wet as Keith's hand roamed down in between her thighs and rubbed her pussy. Breathing accelerated as their lips locked and tongues touched. After two minutes of getting freaky at the stop sign Cognac immediately forced herself to pullback, as her chest palpitated. She wanted to fuck him in the nastiest way.

"Boy, you better stop. We're supposed to be going to the store, remember?" Cognac asked, moving his good feeling hand from in between her legs.

"Aye, that's a nice necklace. When you get that, today?" Keith asked, trying to slickly find out if she had gotten it from dude.

Before Cognac could even respond her eyes widened with terror as she noticed a car racing at top speed in their direction about to T-bone them. She screamed for Keith to hurry up and pull off!! Before Keith could even react to her abrupt looks and actions he turned and looked. The moment was so surreal as Wayne hit the brake, skidding left up alongside of Keith's driver's side door. Keith couldn't pull off fast enough as bullets rained in the car, piercing the door, and ripped through seats as they were getting lit up at point blank range. Keith crashed into a parked car, and Wayne and Loose-Screws sped off into the night. They were left for dead...Keith was slumped against the steering wheel with part of his head and blood splattered on the windshield and dashboard. Cognac tried to open the door and jump out as they were shooting. Unfortunately she was shot twice in the back. With the little energy she had left she managed to climb out the car and fell out on someone's front lawn with blood saturated clothes. Damn, death is so unexpected. Regina and everyone heard the gunfire and ran to the window. They looked down the street and saw a few people who had come out of their homes, mentally blown away by the tragic scene. Regina peered through the window and realized that it was Keith and Cognac involved. Regina yelled "It's Coney!!!" and immediately rushed out of the house as everyone else rushed out behind her. With a face full of tears she darted down the street. She ran over and kneeled next to Cognac, hoping to God she was still alive. With shaky hands, Regina grabbed her cell phone and immediately called nine-one-one! Everybody ran up the street to the incident crying and screaming, traumatized and petrified! Aunt Valerie could barely breathe as she bared witness to a parent's nightmare.

"LORD NOOOOO, NOT MY BABY!!" Aunt Valerie screamed with tears streaming down her face, and covering her mouth with her hands.

"Don't let Eric come over here!" Benita yelled.

Reonna tried to grab Eric before he saw his mother. His heart fluttered as his innocent teary eyes drenched his face.

"Momma! Momma!!!" Eric screamed as he looked on while Reonna carried him back to the house.

Damn...what a way to end the perfect day... This is the exact drama Regina was trying to warn Cognac about... Many times we act off of emotion and not rationality as our hearts desire and pursue what can be more than likely detrimental. It is important to be mindful of the company in which you keep. Karma shows no mercy for those around the one in which it comes for... Never thought we'd be singing amazing grace right after singing Happy Birthday.

...High Speed

The sound of tires squealed as Wayne peeled around multiple corners getting away from the murder scene. At about sixty miles per hour he recklessly drove up residential streets; stop signs didn't mean a muthafuckin thing to him. People who were standing in the street or sitting in their cars felt the concussion in the wind as he blew past them. Eventually he approached a main street and had no choice but to slow up; didn't want to take a chance of getting stopped by the police. Luckily he did because multiple cop cars with their sirens on darted pass as they raced towards the crime scene. Across the street a sign read NO OUTLET FOR THRU TRAFFIC. After the police cars went pass he made a left turn, going in the opposite direction and came to a stop light. Out of the rearview one of the policemen noticed Wayne and saw that the car sort of fit the description of the car that had been reported at the crime scene. So that squad car made a U-turn and accelerated back their way. Wayne looked up in the rearview mirror and saw the squad car approaching but decided to play it cool. He told Loose-Screws to remain ducking down so the police didn't think anything strange. The traffic light had turned green and he carefully pulled off. He kept a natural persona though their hearts thumped fast and hard through their chest. He tried to think positive but the guilt and conviction was tormenting his thoughts every step of the way. He didn't want to break off and look guilty by abruptly turning down a side street so he kept the course. The next traffic light turned red so he came to a stop, and so did the police...directly behind them. He tried to remain cool, but the guilt was killing him, making him feel like the police knew for sure it was them.

"I got two strikes against me already my nigga, I aint about to get another strike and do life in prison." Wayne said, wishing the cops would just pull off and go on about their business.

"Just don't let them see you staring at them or looking nervous." Loose-Screws said, taking a deep breath and thinking to himself that he couldn't believe this shit.

The police put on their lights alerting them to pull over. With a bleak stare, Wayne thought about his life, daughter and family as he reluctantly pulled over just as the light turned green. He knew that he would lose his damn mind if he had to be caged like an animal behind bars and concrete for the rest of his life. Thoughts raced through his mind; he did not want to go out like this... He saw two officers get out of the car with their weapons drawn through the rearview...so he cocked his pistol. At the last second he decided to make a run for it! He threw the car in drive and pulled the fuck off! The officers immediately hopped back in the car and call for back up as they pursued the fugitives. Wayne's nostrils flared, his eyes widened, and his breathing accelerated as he desperately tried to escape. His alert level was high as he violently whipped down numerous streets to get away. The police were on their ass with every turn they made. Loose-Screws was very tense as he hoped they could shake the police off their trail. They ended up making a sharp right turn into traffic as they recklessly drove southbound down Livernois Street, just passing over the Lodge Freeway. Their engines roared as they raced at speeds of almost one-hundred for miles! Davidson road was coming up and they were going too fast to abruptly make a turn or they would lose control and smash directly into a building or something. The light was already green so he tried to mash the petal through the floor to beat the light before it turned back red. The light turned red, and they had about eight seconds before they reached it. Getting caught was not an option...Damn...Wayne chuckled to himself thinking how life can deal you a fucked up hand. And then he said to Loose-Screws... "If we don't make it my nigga, it was real knowing you...And I'll see you on the other side..."

<u>JUST CHILLIN</u>

11:09pm Peaches was chillin at her cousin, Leslie's house with a friend of theirs named Kelly. They sat in lawn chairs around a small circular candle lit table in her backyard having drinks and conversation. On top of the table was a big bottle of 1800 Silver along with three double shot glasses, and an IPod system mildly playing the latest hot tracks. Kelly was having relationship problems with her man, and needed to vent.

"I am so sick of my man right now I do not know what to do. It's like I do all the things a good woman is supposed to do; I cook, I clean, I fuck him good every night or at least every other night. He just won't act right and I'm fed up with him." Kelly expressed and took another shot.

"What is he doing wrong?" Peaches asked.

"Where should I start? I mean, for one, he never tries to apply for a job; he thinks selling weed is all he needs to do. He never helps with any of the chores around the house, I have to do everything myself. He barely gives me money towards the rent or utilities; he takes his little money he makes and go buy clothes and gym shoes." Kelly answered.

"Before I say what I really want to say let me ask you something. Do y'all ever sit down and talk about y'all situation and future? Aint no positive future in drug selling; you either wind up dead or in prison." Leslie stressed.

"I've tried to talk to him plenty of times but it's like talking to the wall. He'll be looking at whatever's on TV or he'll be checking his text messages or face book messages while I'm talking. Then he gets all frustrated when I try to get him to not pay attention to any of that and focus on what I'm saying." Kelly answered, exhaling frustration.

"Well Ima tell you flat out. I aint the one to hate and maliciously try to fuck up someone good relationship, but you need to get rid of him, he's a bum. Why do you put up with a dude like that when its way better dudes out here?" Leslie asked.

Kelly took a deep breath and looked away. She knew that she didn't have any logical reason as of why she was still with this dude because deep down inside she knew it herself that she should've been left him alone. And that's when one of her most ashamed confessions came out "I don't think I'm pretty enough to get something better." Peaches and Leslie both sat up on the edge of their chairs in disbelief of Kelly's response. Peaches had to take another shot of tequila and quickly slammed it.

"Are you serious?! Did I just hear you say that you don't think you're pretty enough to get another man? Girl, I aint trying to be funny but there are thousands of brotha's who would love to be with you, you are beautiful. And just as much as he finds you attractive there are other brotha's that find you just as attractive and will appreciate you that way that you want to be appreciated." Peaches impressed.

"You right....you right. I need to start being more confident, I know." Kelly replied in a very mild tone of voice.

"Look, to hell with all this moping and sad shit. Tonight we're about to go to the club, and hook up with my girls. It's one of my girls birthday party and we gone Celebrate as soon as my child's father comes to pick him up. But for now we are going to have a toast in honor of three strong black women who strive for success, deserve the best, and won't settle for anything less." Peaches said as she poured them another shot.

"Say that shit. I am definitely feeling that statement." Leslie said, smiling at Kelly as they all held their shots in their hand ready to toast.

"Tonight some lucky, handsome, positive, productive, loving black man is going to meet him a gorgeous black woman. And y'all will get to know each other and have major fun, please believe it." Peaches preached.

"Thank ya'll so much, that's why I love y'all. And y'all are right, I do deserve better and I won't settle for someone who doesn't appreciate me. Let us toast." Kelly expressed as they tapped their shot glasses together and simultaneously slammed their shots.

Peaches received a call on her phone and she picked it up off of her lap. She looked at it and saw that it was Antonio then answered it.

"Wsup boo, I mean playa, playa?" Peaches asked in a joking manner.

"I aint no playa, you're the playa. Aye you talked to Regina and them?" Antonio asked.

"Nope, I called about forty-five minutes ago but she aint answering her phone. I called Benita and it's been going straight to her voicemail so I don't know what up with them." Peaches answered.

"Well I just went by her Aunt Valerie house where the surprise party was supposed to be going on, and wasn't nobody there. I didn't see Regina's car, Benita's car or Coney's car. Then I got out and knocked on the door and didn't nobody answer. Wasn't no music playing or nothing." Antonio said.

"Damn, I wonder what the hell is going on with them. Where you at right now?" Peaches asked.

"Just out riding; not too far from your house. You at the crib?" Antonio replied.

"Oh nall, I aint at the crib right now, I'm over Leslie's house, chillin."

"Leslie? Who is Leslie?" Antonio asked.

"You know my cousin Leslie, stay over here off of Tyler Street and Linwood."

"Oh, oh, yeah I remember her. Tell her I said wsup."

"You ought to come through?" Peaches asked, glancing at Leslie and Kelly with a smirk on her face.

"That's cool; I got two of my boys with me though."

"That's perfect because I got two of my girls sitting here chilling with me having a drink." Peaches replied as her girls were all in.

"Okay, what's the address?" Antonio asked as he sipped his drink.

"It's 2456 Tyler. You'll see my car parked in front of her house."

"Alright bet, be there in a few."

"Okay." Peaches replied and hung up.

Peaches immediately called Antonio right back. Antonio answered "Hello?"

"Aye, your boys don't look like monsters do they?" Peaches asked, being silly.

"Nall girl, my partners on point, trust me. You just make sure your girls don't look like something off animal planet."

"Boy Bye! See you when you get here." Peaches said and hung up.

While Peaches and her girls awaited Antonio and his boys to arrive they continued their positive female bonding. They made Kelly feel much better about herself and understand that she could do much better than the man she had. They were big on not bashing all black men and continuing to love and support black men but they definitely were against Kelly's man. In the meantime while they wait it's time to pour up...and have another toast.

STILL CHILLIN

The chrome wheels of Antonio's 2010 Ram Pickup Truck gleamed from the streetlight. In the passenger seat was his main man, Dennis, a well groomed brotha with three-sixty waves, goatee with the Cartier glasses on. In the back seat was his other boy, Terrance. He was a six foot-three, dark-skinned brotha with a well trimmed full beard and nice build. The fella's were cool as a muthafucka; you could find no flaw in their swag. Their heads bobbed in unison as they listened to the music. The sounds weren't too loud, just perfect enough to feel the baseline beating through the body. The smell of cologne and Hennessey pervaded the inside of the ride; in other words these dudes were ready to meet some fine ass sista's. After ten minutes had gone by they finally arrived and parked in front of the house across the street from Leslie's house. Dennis looked over at Antonio "Aye dog, Peaches girls better not be looking hit up, I aint taking one for the team this time."

"She said they aint ugly, so you should be all good." Antonio replied, trying not to laugh.

"Whatever nigga, last time one of your other girls said she had a fine ass friend for me to meet she ended up looking like a muthafuckin Gnu. And then I had to sit there and force myself to entertain her ugly ass while you had fun getting your Mack on with the fine babe." Dennis stressed.

Antonio laughed his ass off because he remembered that night and replied "Aw man, she wasn't that hit up looking."

"This nigga stupid, man what the fuck is a Gnu?" Terrance asked, laughing as well.

"A Gnu is another name for an ugly ass wildebeest." Dennis replied with a straight face.

"Man, you exaggerating...a little." Antonio said, knowing damn well that was some bullshit.

"You a damn lie! It took me a pint of Hennessey and three blunts just to hold me over till it was time for us to go." Dennis impressed.

"But hold up, did you hit it?" Terrance asked.

"Hell nall, man when she took that damn Body Magic off she looked like a busted can of biscuits!" Dennis replied.

"So you mean to tell me she took her clothes off and you aint fuck her?" Terrance asked, thinking he was lying.

"Nigga, hell nall. I told her that the liquor made my blood pressure go up and I had to get my Phlebotomer checked."Dennis replied.

"Nigga, what the fuck is Phlebotomer? It's Phlebotomy. And Phlebotomy is the practice of drawing blood, fool." Antonio replied, shaking his head and laughing.

"So damn what, her ass aint know what I was saying anyway. She thought I was the smartest dude in the D." Dennis replied.

"Aye Terrance, Dennis know he like them gorilla looking ass chicks. Straight silver back Congo looking chicks." Antonio said jokingly.

"Hi, I'm Amy." Terrance replied hilariously referring to the gorilla.

"Nigga, that's yall that like them gorilla's and bears. Y'all don't watch porno's with y'all babes, yall watch animal planet to get in the mood and fuck." Dennis replied.

"Dog, I know you aint talking! You told me you like chicks that look like animals." Antonio replied.

"No I didn't; see now you trying to twist up the story. We were talking about what animal's people would be if they had to be one in the next life. Then we got to saying how everybody looks like or resembles a certain animal and if I had to pick an animal that looked like the type of women I like then it would be cats, and mice." Dennis said.

"Cats and mice?! Man what the fuck is you talking about?" Terrance asked, trying not to laugh too hard.

"Yes muthafucka, cats and mice, but I can't fuck with them chicks that look like birds, ducks, fishes, horses, or otters and shit. Oh, and I damn sure can't fuck with them chicks that look like fucking Avatar's either; big long ass faces and big ass eyes and shit." Dennis expressed with an incredulous look on his face.

They laughed at Dennis's silly ass, and the way he describes things. Antonio pulled his cell phone from the holster and dialed Peaches.

"Hey babe, where yall at?" Peaches asked.

"Just pulled up out front." Antonio answered, looking over at the house.

Immediately Peaches, Leslie, and Kelly screamed their asses off and came running from the backyard and stood on the side of the front porch catching their breath. Antonio and the fellas were looking like what the hell is going on and hopped out the truck. When ladies are looking sexy and in distress fellas always wanna be heroes. Antonio and the fellas walked over to them to see what had happened.

"Damn baby, yall alright?" Antonio asked as they approached Peaches and her girls.

"Hell nall, a big ass family of rats just ran past our asses!" Peaches answered, trying to catch her breath and calm down.

"Aw man, I'm thinking yall were really running from some danger or something." Antonio said like it wasn't nothing to even be afraid of.

"Whatever, but since you so damn brave why don't you go back there and get our drink then." Peaches sarcastically suggested.

Antonio scoffed at her little suggestion and asked "What, I'm supposed to be scured."

Antonio walked into the backyard and grabbed the bottle of 1800 off of the table and noticed a rat dart into the drain hole in the ground by the garage. He walked over to the whole and looked down in it.

"Man, this y'all little rat problem? Y'all should've been handled this." Antonio said.

"Yeah, I tried to get my uncle over here to take care of the problem but he just aint came through yet." Leslie said as she and the rest of them kind of eased back there.

"Man, you can take care of this problem yo damn self." Antonio said like it wasn't shit to it.

"Well since you such a rat expert why don't you get them up out of there? You know how to do it?" Leslie asked.

"Yeah, if you got some gasoline around here in a gas can." Antonio answered, looking around.

"It should be a gas can right there in the garage on that shelf to the right." Leslie said as she carefully eased back there a little more, looking in the garage from afar.

Antonio walked into the garage and grabbed the gas can. He shook it a little bit making sure it had enough gas in it. He walked over to the hole and removed the cap. He gladly poured gas down the drain saturating the rats. He felt his pockets to see if he had a lighter and thought about it; he needed a match.

"Which one of y'all got some matches?" Antonio asked.

"I got some for you my nigga." Dennis answered as he walked over to Antonio trying to impress the ladies as well.

Once Dennis handed him the matches he uttered "I see you over there looking at Leslie big round ass."

"Hell yeah, Ima try to tap that." Dennis replied.

"Aye, yall aint supposed to be over there whispering and shit. Y'all supposed to be handling them rats." Peaches said.

"Anna-May, keep ya mouth shut and let Big Daddy handle this." Antonio retorted.

Antonio tore one of the matches out of the booklet. He squatted down a little to make sure he didn't miss the hole when he threw the match in there. Then the moment came "TAKE THIS BITCHES!!!" Antonio said as he struck the match and threw it down in the hole! Immediately a fat hairy ass rat that was on fire came shooting up out of the drain squealing like a muthafucka and landed on Antonio's chest. The rats claws were hooked in his shirt. "FUCK!!!" Dennis yelled as he jumped back trying to get out of the way. "OH MY GOD, GET IT OFF ME!!!!" Antonio screamed like a bitch as he tried to shake it off. He didn't really want to touch it especially since it was on fire! Antonio was shaking the hell out his shirt, falling all up against the gate, wishing the Lord would make the rat get off of him. He started fumbling his way over to where Peaches and them where standing. "BOY, GET THE FUCK AWAY FROM US WITH THAT THANG ON YOU!!" Peaches yelled, damn near falling to the ground as they ran back a few steps. They were dying laughing as they tried to think of what to do to help him. Dennis saw a hard plastic rake with a wooden handle in the garage and grabbed it. "HOLD STILL MY NIGGA, I GOT YOU!" Dennis yelled strongly and swung the rake hard as hell and slapped the shit out of Antonio in the head. "Man what the fuck is you doing, you stupid fuck?!" Antonio asked, trying to stop from getting ate alive by the rat and his ass whooped with a big ass rake. "My bad dog, I just don't want that rat to get on me though, I just got this shirt. Just be still so I can get it off." Dennis said, finally swiping the rat, causing it to shake loose and run. Peaches and Leslie had tears in their eyes because they were laughing so damn hard, and could barely catch their breath. "Oh my

God that was the funniest shit I've ever seen!" Terrance said, holding his stomach while he was on the ground laughing. Kelly thought she was going to pee on herself because she was laughing her ass off. Antonio pulled his collar, looking inside of his shirt to see if the rat had scratched him. Dennis sat the rake down and walked over to him, trying his best not to laugh. "You alright, dog?" Dennis asked, trying to hold a straight face. Antonio looked up at Dennis and saw his lip trembling, trying not to laugh. "I know you aint about to laugh at me too after you just beat my ass with that rake?" Antonio asked as he just looked at him. Dennis didn't want to laugh at his boy in front of the babes, but that fiery ass rat leaping on his chest was funny as damn hell. Dennis was holding a straight face but because Antonio was staring at him it was making it too hard to hold back. Dennis had the stupidest look on his face as he bit down on his teeth and tried tightening his jaw but the pressure was just too much. Dennis turned around and bust out laughing his ass off with everyone else.

"It's all good, I got y'all asses. I promise you I'm laughing my ass off as soon as y'all fuck up." Antonio said as he walked over to them.

"Aw boo, don't be mad. Momma gone take care of you. Here, come in the house so I can take a good look at you." Peaches said as she grabbed Antonio by the hand, leading him into the house.

"I got a first aid kit in the medicine cabinet over the sink in the bathroom." Leslie said, as she tried to calm herself down from laughing.

"While we're doing this, why don't yall introduce y'all selves? We'll be right back." Peaches suggested.

Peaches cell phone rang as she was walking in the house. She looked at it and saw that it was Regina calling and answered as she doctored on Antonio... Damn...as if things couldn't get worse.

DETROIT RECEIVING CARE HOSPITAL

Aunt Valerie, Regina and everyone sat impatiently in the hospital lobby waiting on the Doctor to come talk to them. Everyone tried to remain positive and hopeful though their nervousness was evident. Regina was so damn nervous but also mad because she told Cognac something like this could happen if she kept messing around with those type dudes...but her hard headed ass didn't want to listen. Aunt Valerie was doing her best to remain calm but her slightly trembling legs and nervous hands showed that she had a problem with doing so. The thought of Keith being pronounced dead at the scene of the crime did not make matters anymore promising. Antonio and Peaches walked in and approached the information desk acquiring about Cognac. The clerk told them that they had to go wait in the lobby for now. Just as soon as they noticed Aunt Valerie and everyone and went over to talk to them is when the Doctor came out. The Doctor had a plain dry looking face as he approached them. Regina stood up hoping the Doctor would provide positive information, but the dry look on his face was making it hard not to think negative.

"Please tell me you have some good news." Regina said as her heart thumped a little harder and was full of hope.

Everyone else stood up wishing, and praying the Doctor says the things they want to hear.

"Cognac is going to be fine, but she's definitely lost a significant amount of blood and going to experience some discomfort and pain. She was shot twice in the back but we opted not to remove the bullets." Doctor Williams said.

"You opted not to remove the bullets?!!" Aunt Valerie retorted.

"Yes, the reason we opted not to remove the bullets is because one of them is paralleled with her spine and if we try to remove it then it's a sixty-five percent chance that she could be paralyzed. The other bullet is positioned just above the kidney and if we try to remove it there's a strong possibility that the bullet can dislodge and be fatal." Doctor Williams explained.

Men-Tal

"Oh my God, I can't believe this. Cynthia has been in a coma for the last eight months and now my cousin. I can't believe this." Regina deeply replied, covering her mouth with her hand.

"Rochelle will be fine; she just needs plenty of rest so that she can make a great recovery. Don't over stress yourselves about it, think positive. These things happen all the time. She'll be alright, just keep her off of her feet and well rested." Doctor Williams answered in a comforting manner.

"Can we all go back there and see her?" Aunt Valerie asked.

"Yes, but unfortunately only two people will be allowed to go back at a time." Doctor Williams replied.

"Okay, that's fine. Me and my Aunt will go back." Regina replied.

"Okay follow me." Doctor Williams said as she led them through the hospital doors.

The hallways smelled like sickness as they walked through. A nurse pushed a rolling cart filled with meals from door to door, it was feeding time. They arrived at room one-hundred and seven, the doctor opened the door and they walked in. The sound of the heart monitor pulsated as

Cognac lied there fighting to get better. The sight of her lying there was disheartening though the doctor assured that she'll be okay. Aunt Valerie and Regina walked over to her feeling deeply as Aunt Valerie gently rubbed her hand.

"Is she sleep, Doctor Williams?" Aunt Valerie asked, looking down at Cognac with compassion.

"She's in what we call an induced coma. We had to do so in order to stabilize her so that the bullets didn't dislodge. But I assure you that she'll be fine." Doctor Williams said.

"How long will the coma last?" Regina asked.

"It can take a week, it can take two weeks, but she'll have to remain in the coma until she recovers." Doctor Williams answered.

Aunt Valerie and Regina were okay with the results, just hoping for a successful recovery. Regina put her arm around Aunt Valerie's back and gently leaned her head against Aunt Valerie's head as they looked upon Cognac. Let this...be a lesson learned.

MOTOR CITY JAVA HOUSE

12:37pm the next day Regina, Benita, and Peaches were having lunch at the Motor City Java House just next door to a place called the Artist Village. They ordered three Jamaican Me Crazy coffees, three turkey sandwiches, and Benita and Regina had purchased a piece of Mr. Vegaz's famous strawberry cheesecake as well. They hadn't eaten since last night at the party so they were starving. They looked up at the wall mounted television and paid very close attention as the local news gave the latest reports.

"I am so damn tired right now. I can just lay my head down on this table and go to sleep right here." Benita said.

"I feel you on that, because I promise you when I get home I'm cutting off my phone, closing all the blinds and getting me some good ass sleep." Peaches replied.

"Hell yeah, you and me both. Last night made it official that I'm taking me a vacation. I'ma pack my clothes and go to a nice hotel, get me a massage every day, and just relax in the spa." Regina added as she put another fork of cheesecake in her mouth.

"Damn, that sounds good right about now." Benita replied as she reached over her shoulder, massaging the back of her neck to relieve some tension.

"Hell yeah, after that crazy shit last night I just want to block everything out and evaluate my life and the people in it." Peaches said, briefly glancing at the TV screen.

"I mean, what the hell? Why would somebody just come shoot them up like that? People have literally lost their minds now days." Benita said.

"I think somebody had it out for ole boy if you ask me." Regina answered.

"I think so too. I just don't see someone wanting to kill Cognac personally. She aint even out here like that. " Peaches said.

"I know, right." Benita replied.

"UNLESS...unless...it was another person in the picture that wasn't happy with the way things were going..." Regina insinuated.

"Another person? You think him or her was seeing somebody else on the side?" Peaches asked as she leaned forward ready to hear something juicy.

"I don't know about him but I know she was. Her and I just had a conversation about this the other night. She told me that the other guy was a little too much for her and she was going to let him know that she was going to stop seeing him." Regina said, swigging her coffee.

"Ooohhhh, so you talking about some ole fatal attraction type stuff going on, huh?" Benita asked with a straight face and eyes widened.

"You ever met this guy she was seeing?" Peaches asked.

"Yeah, matter of fact we all met him at the same time at the New Years Eve Ball." Regina said.

"Wait a minute, you talking about ole boy that was buying us the food and drinks?" Peaches asked with an incredulous look on her face.

"Yup, that's exactly who I'm talking about." Regina replied.

"Oh yeah, I remember him! YOU THINK HE DID IT?" Benita asked in a very loud voice.

"Girl, calm down, your ass loud as hell... No, I'm not saying that he did it; I'm just saying that he was the other guy she was seeing." Regina replied.

"Oh yeah, now it's coming back to me! He was the dude that got into it with Keith that night." Peaches recalled.

"Yup, and she was dating both of them." Regina replied.

"SO, she was single and she could date who she wanted to date." Benita stated.

"Yeah, but you gotta be careful now days, because people aint playing no games with their feelings and emotions. A person will kill you now days if they feel like you getting over on them for their money, energy and time and don't appreciate them enough to be with them. And we can say all day long about how it aint right but guess what, we hear about a murder-suicide almost every other week. So it's best that people take that into consideration when their out here dating folks." Regina preached.

"Damn Gina, you make me wanna fingerprint a brotha and do a background check on him before I even give him my number." Peaches said, being funny.

"Ya think." Benita replied.

"The one thing that we have been absolutely misled about is that men don't have feelings and emotions. That doesn't make a bit of sense because if that was true then these dudes wouldn't care or get mad no matter what a woman does. And some of us believe in that ole dumb teaching and call our men punks, bitches and belittling them until they can't take no more and react in a violent manner." Regina said.

"Yeah, but aint no man got no business putting their hands on a woman." Peaches replied.

"And that's where we mislead ourselves and our young daughters. We teach them that a man shouldn't put his hands on a woman, but we never teach the woman that she should never put her hands on a man. And that very same teaching subconsciously makes some women think that it's okay for her to hit him but he aint supposed to hit her back. If we stop teaching that old dumb cliché then I guarantee you it will help reduce domestic violence a little more." Regina preached.

"Yeah, but I still say that a man should never put his hands on a woman." Peaches replied.

"Peaches, a relationship isn't only about you. You have to consider your mates feelings as well. There's nothing wrong with teaching that men AND women shouldn't put their hands on each other in a violent manner, period. Yo ass just don't want to teach that because it makes you have to calm yo hostile emotions down." Regina said.

"Peaches, Regina is right. Your ass know you can be off the hook sometimes too. However both y'all ass can never stay focused on one subject at a time. Now I'm trying to figure out if ole boy had something to do with Coney getting shot." Benita said, reestablishing direction in the conversation.

"You right, we did get way the hell off the subject. But look, like I was saying. I aint trying to say that it was him that shot them up but I damn show aint X-ing out no possibilities till we find out who it was that did it, and why." Regina stated as she took the last bite of her cheesecake.

They ate the rest of their food as they watched the news, and listened to the next breaking story reported by news caster Albert Allen. "Hi, this is Albert Allen coming to you live from the fatal car crash scene that claimed the lives of four people last night resulting from a high-speed chase. Around eleven-fifteen last night Officer Tom Jeeter and his partner James Morton attempted to pull a couple of young men over. The officer put the flashers on, signaling for them stop and pull to the side of the road. When the officers got out of the car and approached the vehicle the driver put the car in gear and sped off. The officers got back in their car and pursued the fugitives down residential streets which led to them driving at over a hundred miles per hour going south up Livernois Road. They chased the fugitives for miles before the young man attempted to flee through the red light at the busy Davidson Road intersection. The officers reported that once the light turned red the suspects accelerated trying to beat the traffic and that's when they rammed into a car, killing two people inside of it. The suspects spun out of control and smashed into another car critically injuring the driver. The two suspects were both pronounced dead at the scene. It is also reported that the police recovered two hand guns from the vehicle the suspects were driving in. This is all the information we have for now. This is Albert Allen reporting."

<u>*WANTED*</u>

Michelle stood in front of her bathroom mirror combing her hair, getting ready to go have brunch with a guy she met named Maurice. She swooped hair over her right eye adding a bit more sex appeal. She picked her eyeliner up off of the sink and carefully traced her eyelid, leaving a sharp point at the outer edge. Then she picked up her lip gloss and drew around her lips making them look deliciously sweet and sticky; you couldn't tell her a muthafuckin thing. She popped her lips and turned to the side, making sure her jeans were riding her ass nice and tight. She left out the bathroom and walked into the kitchen, grabbing her cell phone, keys, and purse off of the counter. She saw that she had missed Maurice's call and immediately called him back. She loved the tone of his masculine voice, and as long as he kept speaking the right words she loved to hear she was going to be happily fucking the shit out of him real soon. He answered, and she was all smiles and laughter. She headed to the side door, about to go meet him at the restaurant; she couldn't wait to see him. She opened the door, and immediately got the piss scared out of her as Demarco stepped in breathing heavy and looking paranoid.

"Get the fuck off the phone, I gotta talk to you." Demarco said sincerely with a scowl on his face.

"Damn nigga, what the fuck is up with you? And why you breathing so hard like somebody after you or something?" Michelle asked, panting and trying to catch her breath.

Demarco never responded to her question as he glanced outside once more making sure no police had seen him walk in and then he shut the door behind him.

"Tell that nigga you'll call him back." Demarco said as he made his way up the small staircase and into her kitchen.

Michelle just looked at him like she couldn't believe this nigga was interrupting her plans. She told Maurice she would call him back and hung up the phone. She shook her head and walked up the stairs and into the kitchen. She didn't see him so she walked to the den where she saw him standing by the TV picking up the remote control.

"Okay, would you like to tell me what the hell is going on, Mr. Demarco?" Michelle asked and then looked at him with an eyebrow raised and mouth partly opened.

"Man, just look and stop trippin." Demarco replied as he turned on the TV.

He flipped through a couple channels till he got to one with the local news showing. The news was re-airing the story, showing the violent car accident and deaths of Wayne, Loose-Screws, and the other casualties involved. They also elaborated on how the guns that were retained from the car wreck were the guns that were used in the shooting death of Keith and the shooting of Cognac before she was rushed to the hospital. They also explained how the text messages in Wayne's phone instructed him to kill Cognac and Keith which ultimately led to fugitive number one...Demarco. They showed a picture of Demarco on the screen, and he looked at it for a few seconds and turned off the TV. Michelle stood there for a few seconds in aw with her mouth open.

"Are you serious? Oh my God, I can't believe them niggas is fucking dead, man. Why did you let this bitch push you to this point?" Michelle asked, frustrated about the drama.

"Look, I know, I can't take the shit back. It's too fuckin late for me to boo hoo now. They just gone have to catch me." Demarco said with a straight face, and sat down on her couch.

"Damn nigga, so what you gone do now?" Michelle asked as she sat down on the couch as well.

Demarco peeped through the blinds, glancing outside and then looked back at her and replied "I don't know, but what you got to eat around this muthafucka, I'm starving?"

LESSON WELL LEARNED

A week later Cognac lied on her elevated hospital bed watching TV, flipping through the channels. She had awakened from her coma earlier that morning, and couldn't wait to get the hell up out of there. The sun was beaming outside, and the weather was perfect, making you want to go out and enjoy life. She was wishing the doctor would come in any moment and tell her she was going to be discharged, but that was highly unlikely. Slightly frustrated that nothing worth watching was on TV, she turned the volume down and lied the remote down on the side of the bed. She closed her eyes, vaguely recalling what had happened the night of her birthday. She remembered being at the party with everyone laughing and smiling. She remembered her and Keith leaving out to go to the store, and talking to Aunt Val and Eric in front of the house. She remembered talking to Keith while they were at the stop sign.....her heart slightly accelerated as she recalled the beaming headlights coming in their direction. She remembered the puzzled look on Keith's face...just before the loud scream of the tires skidding as Wayne's car swerved up next to them... just before the borage of bullets ripped through the car...just before she desperately tried to open the door and escape death. Three slight knocks on the door caught her attention, taking her out of her horrific daydream. She said come in and the door knob turned and the door opened. Regina, Benita, and Peaches walked in with helium balloons and get well cards. Cognac smiled pleasantly as they entered.

"Hey sweetie!" Regina said as she walked over to Cognac and gave her a kiss on the cheek.

"Hey y'all. I'm starting to think y'all love me or something." Cognac said jokingly with a smile, just happy that they were there.

"Girl, don't geek yourself up, I just didn't have nothing else to do, so here you go." Benita replied humorously as she leaned over and kissed Cognac on the cheek and sat some flowers by her bed.

"Hey girl, I'm glad to see you getting better." Peaches said as she approached her with a smile.

"Thank you, boo." Cognac replied with a smile.

"So when are they going to let you go home?" Peaches asked.

"I wish I was going home today but more than likely their going to keep me here so they can monitor me over night and make sure I don't slip back into a coma." Cognac replied.

"Well as bad as we want you home we definitely want you to be okay, first." Peaches said.

"That's right." Regina concurred.

"It aint right if our girl aint tight." Benita added.

Regina handed Cognac the Get Well cards that each one of them had bought for her. One by one she read them and was sincerely touched by every word that was written. Before she finished reading the last card her face straightened and a tear trickled from her eye. She sniffed as she tightened the corners of her lips, and wiped her face. Regina, Benita and Peaches gathered around her bed and hugged her. Aint nothing like the consoling feeling of sisterly love, and support. Cognac gathered herself and wiped her face with her hands and said "I don't know what I would do without y'all. And Regina, I know I should have listened to you when you tried to warn

me and this mess would've never happened...
I was so stupid."

"Girl bye, this aint even about to be a beat
up on Cognac party; we all make mistakes.
Aint none of us perfect; we just gotta learn
from our mistakes and do our best to better
ourselves." Regina replied.

Regina's cell phone rang so she grabbed
it, looked at it and saw that it was Sarah
Langston. She answered the phone and Sarah
asked to speak to Cognac. With a smile,
Regina handed Cognac the phone. Cognac
was curious about who it was as she grabbed
it. She looked at the caller I.D. and smiled
then put it to her ear.

"Hey Sarah." Cognac said, happily.

"Hey sweetie, how you feeling?" Sarah
Langston asked.

"I'm fine, just can't wait to go home."
Cognac said with a pleasant smile.

"You will, just take it easy when you do.
But not only do I want you to take it easy on
yourself physically, but I want you to take it
easy mentally and emotionally. And stop
being so hard on yourself. You have to
understand that it is okay for you to forgive
yourself for your mistakes; no ones perfect.
Just remember everything happens for a

reason. Just make sure you learn from it." Sarah Langston expressed.

"You never cease to amaze me with your wisdom and how you just know certain things without me even saying anything." Cognac replied.

"You don't have to say it; I can hear it all in your voice. You're a beautiful person inside and out, and I just want you to be happy...you deserve it." Sarah Langston replied.

"Thank you, Sarah. I love you." Cognac replied, glancing at Regina.

"I love you to. Well look, Regina already told me that she and the girls were coming up there to see you so I'm going to let them enjoy you, and I will talk to you tomorrow." Sarah Langston said.

"Okay." Cognac said.

"Alright sweetie, you take care and be safe." Sarah Langston said as she hung up the phone.

Cognac hit the end button and handed the phone back to Regina. Peaches and Benita went out and picked up some delicious food from a restaurant. They knew that Cognac would love to have something to grub on other than that bland hospital food they were serving her. They also grabbed some juices to drink and a couple of magazines so she could read later on when she was by herself. They didn't want her stressing over the drama that happened on her birthday. So they ate, drank, laughed and talked about the latest happenings that were going on up at the salon. Damn, it feels good to know that you have true friends that really got your back in your time of need. About thirty minutes later the girls took off and left.

Shortly afterwards there was a knock at the door and a voice asked "Is it okay to come in?" Cognac looked towards the door and replied "Yes, you can come in." The door opened and the doctor entered the room. He walked over to the bed with his clipboard in hand and introduced himself "Hello my name is Dr. Vida, and I'll be filling in for Dr. Morgan. I need to check you out real quick and make sure you're okay." "Okay." Cognac replied. Dr. Vida had Cognac sit up in the bed so that he could listen to her breathing. He put his stethoscope in his ears and gently placed the diaphragm on her back and told her to breathe in and out. He was satisfied with how she was breathing but still wanted to monitor her for the remainder of the day and more than likely discharger her tomorrow.

"So how does my breathing sound?" Cognac asked.

"You sound fine. You are a very blessed woman; the average person isn't able to survive deadly shots like that. The Most High showed mercy on you because one of the bullets was less than an inch away from striking your spine and possibly causing paralysis." Dr. Vida impressed.

"Oh my God." Cognac said, startled by the news.

"But you're okay though, you just need plenty of rest." Dr. Vida assured.

"Thank you Dr. Vida." Cognac replied.

"You're very welcome. I'll be back in here later to check on you."

"Okay." Cognac replied and then the doctor left the room.

BUSINESS AND PLEASURE

Another day at the salon and everyone seemed to be in beautiful spirits this sunny afternoon. Regina was in her office handling Essential Beauty Salon's paper work. Benita and De'Juan were wiping down their hydraulic chairs and cleaning their areas preparing for their next clients. Antonio's area was slightly adjacent from Peaches area where he was sterilizing his foot spa getting it nice and clean. Peaches had just finished washing her client's hair in the washroom and had brought her out and placed her under the dryer. Peaches walked back to her area and sat down in her hydraulic chair, picked up a magazine and started reading it. A two-thousand and twelve Mercedes Benz pulled up and parked in front of the salon. The driver's door opened and a ladies pretty foot in a gold designer flip flop stepped out. She reached over in the passenger seat and grabbed her purse. She got out of the car shutting the door behind her, and locked it with the remote. Her hair was fly and sexy, flowing down to her shoulders. Her stunner shades commanded attention, displaying boldness, and confidence. Her lip-gloss made her lips look tasty and delicious as wine-candy. Her walk was hypnotizing as her hips swayed in her curve riding Baby Phat jeans. Damn, this chick was fuckin sexy. Peaches noticed her approaching and was curious about who she was coming to see being that her hair was already done. She kept her magazine up to her face and glanced at Antonio from the side to see if he was looking at her. Antonio was in his own world getting his area prepped and had no clue someone was approaching. De'Juan and Benita did a double take when they saw her. The lady walked in and Peaches took it upon herself to greet her.

"Hello, how are you doing, can I help you?" Peaches asked very politely.

"Yes, I have an appointment with Antonio." Marvelisa answered as she looked around admiring the salon.

Antonio heard his name and turned around and looked. "Oh hey Marvelisa, you're right on time, go ahead and have a seat."

"Thank you sweetie." Marvelisa replied as she sat down.

Peaches noticed Marvelisa called him sweetie. She wondered if they had anything going on before; after all Marvelisa was undeniably attractive. Peaches went to go get her client from under the dryer. Antonio had Marvelisa role her pants legs up a little, and place her feet in the spa. Peaches had her client come sit in her hydraulic chair and started doing her hair. After letting Marvelisa's feet soak long enough Antonio sat down in his chair in front of her and took a towel and started drying her feet. Marvelisa closed her eyes and smiled as she enjoyed her feet being pampered. Peaches noticed how extra pleasured Marvelisa looked as Antonio did her cuticles. Peaches loved Antonio but never told him. She always stressed that she wasn't ready for a serious relationship, but it was bothering her to see this sexy lady enjoying Antonio's touch. Even though Antonio was simply doing his job, in Peaches mind he was passionately caressing her feet. Peaches knew Antonio had a foot fetish and to her it looked like he was enjoying it...a little too much. He started gently scrubbing her feet to get off any dead skin. Marvelisa slightly moaned "Mm mm mm" as Antonio took the file and started carefully stroking her toes. When no one was looking Peaches took one of her small plastic combs and threw it, hitting Antonio in the back.

"Owww." Antonio responded to the hit, looking back like what the hell.

Peaches sneered at him and kept doing her clients hair. Antonio turned around and continued doing Marvelisa's feet. He started massaging them and Marvelisa exhaled with pleasure as her toes seemed to be pointing for his lips. Peaches really wanted to go over there and tell her "BITCH, all that damn moaning and enjoyment aint even necessary". Marvelisa moved her body a little, getting in a little more comfortable position and said "Your hands feel so damn good right now. I could just marry you." Antonio chuckled and replied "Just trying to do a good service." "And indeed you are serving me very well." Marvelisa replied. Peaches took a penny out of her purse and threw it at him, hitting him in the back. She looked down at her clients head as he turned around again and looked. He knew the only reason she was trippin is because Marvelisa was attractive...very attractive. He turned back around and continued. Peaches grabbed her phone off of the counter and started typing real quickly. Antonio's phone chimed letting him know he had a text message. He grabbed his phone out of his side holster and looked at the message from Peaches that read "I'm gone kick yo ass!" Antonio replied back "Y?" Peaches heard her phone chime indicating she had a message but purposely didn't even look at it. De'Juan and Benita finished up their clients and took a nice lunch break since they didn't have any more clients for another hour. Antonio gave her a French manicure that looked astounding. Marvelisa twirled her feet, admiring how beautiful Antonio had them looking. Antonio hooked her hands up as well and had her feeling simply stunning when he was done. She reached inside of her purse and pulled out some money then paid him.

"Hold on let me give you your change." Antonio said.

"Oh, I'm fine sweetie, it's yours." Marvelisa replied.

Antonio looked at her "You do know this is a fifteen dollar tip you're leaving me?"

"I know sweetie, you're well worth the tip." Marvelisa said, giving him the sexy eyes.

"Well, thank you, Lisa." Antonio replied, placing the money in his pocket.

"Well, Ima get on out of here. Please put me down for an appointment next week at the same time." Marvelisa said as she headed towards the door, smiling.

"Alright, will do." Antonio said as Marvelisa left out.

Antonio turned around and sterilized the foot spa and wiped down his chair. Peaches had just finished up on her client, and had her looking superb. While the lady was paying Peaches Antonio walked to the backroom. Peaches client left and then she locked the door behind her. She didn't have any other clients coming anytime soon and she hoped that Antonio didn't either. She turned and headed for the backroom as well. She walked in and Antonio was leaning back up against the counter drinking a strawberry kiwi juice. Peaches just stood there and looked at him with a straight face. She walked up on him and stood directly in front of him, looking in his eyes.

"What did I do that got you wanting to beat up on me this time little lady?" Antonio asked as he looked off to the right and exhaled in frustration.

Peaches sneered at him and then took his juice out of his hand and sat it on the counter. She stepped all the way up on him with her body touching his. Antonio looked at her with a puzzling look on his face. She gently cuffed the back of his head and pulled him closer and sensually kissed his lips. She started rubbing his dick making it get rock hard and bulge through his pants. She started kissing on his neck and rubbing his dick a little harder. She unzipped his pants and reached inside and juggled his balls. She gripped his dick and pulled it out. She started kissing his chest and stroking his shaft. She got down on her knees and sniffed his balls; the natural scent of his dick and nuts made her wet and hot in the ass. She was on a mission to suck the fuck out of his dick and have him bang her ass doggy-style before Benita and De'Juan came back. She puckered her lips on the tip of his dick, and sucked it sensually. She slowly deep-throated it as far as she could get it in. She fiercely started spitting and sucking all on his dick WHEN ALL OF A SUDDEN!...the door opened up. Benita stepped in, caught off guard looking like WHAT THE FUCK! She was trippin out as she looked at Peaches down on her knees facing him while he looked up at her with a surprised look on his face.

"What the hell yall doing?!" Benita could only ask with a surprised look on her face.

"What you mean? Oh, um, she's fixing my um...zipper....it broke." Antonio said as Peaches immediately put his dick back in his pants.

"And she had to be down on her knees to fix your zipper, huh?" Benita asked with her face looking like yeah right.

"Yeah, that's only because I was down on my knees praying right before he walked up on me." Peaches replied and stood up.

Benita just looked at them with a face full of sarcasm and replied "Y'all going to hell."

KINKY ROOTS

An hour and a half later Regina had showed up to the salon and started styling her client, Mrs. Holland's hair. Regina loved doing her hair because she was always sweet and had something motivating, and positive to say. Regina was looking at Mrs. Holland's face through the side mirror that was mounted on the wall. She truly admired her beauty.

"Mrs. Holland, you are so beautiful." Regina said with a pleasant smile.

Mrs. Holland smiled so pleasant and overjoyed then replied "Why, thank you Mrs. Regina, you just made an old lady's day."

"Well, that's because you always make my day every time you come here and sit in my chair." Regina said, sincerely with a smile.

"Thank you sweetie; I love enjoying life and seeing people smile. My husband told me I was the sunshine of his life and I brightened his every single day. And ever since I've always liked making others smile." Mrs. Holland said.

"That is so beautiful. I love hearing about beautiful love like that." Regina said.

"Thank you, sweetie." Mrs. Holland said.

"Mrs. Holland?"

"Yes, sweetie?"

"If I'm not getting to personal, may I ask how old are you?"

"Seventy-two and counting." Mrs. Holland said proudly.

"ARE YOU SERIOUS?! You are so gorgeous, Mrs. Holland. I pray that I'm blessed to look as beautiful as you when I get you age. You don't look anywhere near seventy-two." Regina said in amazement.

"Thank you Regina... You know...I hope my granddaughter turns out to be beautiful and smart just like you."

Regina felt honored and replied "Thank you Mrs. Holland."

Regina smiled as she continued laying Mrs. Holland's hair. De'Juan was working on a ladies eyebrows; he concentrated and focused as he arched them with precision. Antonio was creatively designing his client's nails with playing card symbols such as hearts, diamonds, clubs, and spades. Peaches was just about done braiding her clients hair, and Benita was wiping down her chair preparing for her client Ms. Jasmine who had just pulled up outside. Sitting in the waiting section to get their hair done were DeAndrea and Kenya. They were thumbing through a Hip Hop magazine checking out the latest gossip. They both looked up, captivated by Jasmine's looks. She stood five foot five with pretty sun-kissed skin. She had a beautiful fluffy afro that you just want to run your fingers through, and hips, thighs, and booty for days.

"Wsup girl?!" Benita said as she walked up to Jasmine and hugged her.

"Hey boo." Jasmine replied with a smile.

"I love your fro, girl I'm thinking about rocking one myself this winter." Benita said as she reached up and touched Jasmines hair.

"I know it will look good on you. And you can switch it up and rock the braids to."

"Let me get everything situated real quick so I can go ahead and wash it for you."

"Alright, well I'm about to sit down over here." Jasmine replied.

"Okay." Benita replied as she walked to the washroom to get the sink ready.

DeAndrea and Kenya just looked at Jasmine enviously as she walked by to sit down. They continued flipping through the magazine and would frequently glance over at her. Jasmine had picked up one of the magazines off of the table and started looking through it. Through her peripheral vision Jasmine noticed DeAndrea looking at her. She looked up and briefly caught DeAndrea starring at her all weird and then quickly putting her head down. Jasmine blew it off as nothing and continued reading the article in the magazine. Once again she noticed DeAndrea looking at her and it was getting irritating. Jasmine quickly looked up at her with a serious face and decided to address her.

"Excuse me, but do I know you?" Jasmine asked as a couple of people took notice to the tension by the tone of her voice.

"No you don't know me. I was just looking at your afro; it's a lot of hair." DeAndrea replied.

"Ooookay...Ima take that as a compliment, thank you." Jasmine said with an eyebrow raised and continued looking at the article.

"I know you thank God for the relaxer and the straightening comb. How long it take you to straighten all that and get that Dime

Diva look?" DeAndrea asked as she looked at her fro with a stank ass look on her face.

"First, what makes you think I'm here to straighten my hair?" Jasmine asked, incredulously.

"Well, don't get all testy, I just didn't think nobody really felt that rockin the Angela Davis look or the Dr. J look was sexy."

"It's obvious my sista that you've been successfully detached from your ethnicity. I don't have to throw a bunch of chemicals and fire in my head for men to like me. I don't have to straighten my hair out in order for me to feel beautiful, sexy, A DIME DIVA, find a man, or to feel confident about my looks in public. I'm happy with the way God made me. And as far as the Dr. J thing you tried to slide in there; he'll be the furthest thing from a man's mind when he's with me. He'll be too busy focused on my mind, my lips, my thick hips and round ass, trust me." Jasmine retorted impressively.

"See, that's what's wrong with y'all soul sista wanna-bee's. Just because I get my hair pressed don't mean I don't like my African roots or my ethnit-whatever that shit you just said. And trust me, I can get a man." DeAndrea said nastily.

"Yeah, but the problem is you can't keep one because you don't have no substance worth sticking around for." Jasmine replied nasty right back at her.

"I got all the substance a nigga need. I don't know what the fuck you talking about!"

"Whatever, you probably one of them Brewster Project mentality having, tack head facebook chicks posting pictures of your babies lying in money which is so fucking ignorant. You dress like a hoe and a real man don't want a hoe as his woman or wife. And you wonder why females like you got three and four different baby Daddy's. It's just like prostitution; they fuck you and get the hell on. And based off of your character that's the only caliber of dudes you can get." Jasmine said, getting pissed.

Even though Jasmine was just randomly throwing out low blow scenarios it had DeAndrea shocked because Jasmines words hit the nail right on the head. She stood up and paused for a hot second and all she could do was reply "Bitch, you don't know me!"

"Bitch you need to check yoself!" Kenya said as she stood up pointing her finger at Jasmine.

"Hold up, just because I'm conscious, my sistas don't mean I won't whoop both of y'all asses if I have to." Jasmine said as she put the magazine down and stood up.

By that time Regina and the rest of the staff walked over to resolve the situation and make sure it didn't escalate. Peaches and Antonio stood in front of DeAndrea and Kenya trying to calm them down. Benita stood in front of Jasmine to calm her as well. Other clients were looking like what the hell, thinking the drama was about to jump off. Regina raised her voice and got their attention.

"Excuse me, EXCUSE ME, please calm down, ladies. We're trying to run a successful business here." Regina said as Kenya butted in with a nasty disposition.

"You aint gone whoop shit, bitch!" Kenya yelled.

"Aw, now your lil dike friend wanna step up like a man and protect you." Jasmine said sarcastically.

"Bitch, I'm man enough to bend your ass over and fuck you better than your man can, bitch!" Kenya yelled ignorantly.

"See that's where your little confused, dumb, wanna be a man ass is wrong. You can be attracted to pussy all you want, and lick it all you want but the fact still remains that YOU WILL NEVER EVER EXPERIENCE WHAT PUSSY ACTUALLY FEELS LIKE BECAUSE YOU DON'T HAVE A DICK, STUPID! And you can buy all the dildo's you want but they will never allow you the ultimate feeling and pleasure of a dick being in a pussy." Jasmine logically preached as some of the clients that looked on started clapping.

There was no logical reply for Kenya to respond with so she just blurted out with fired up emotions and her fist balled up. "I hate you! Bitch, die!"

"Well, we're all going to experience that one day so you could've saved that little juvenile remark. However, it's obvious the truth hurts… and aint shit you can do about it!" Jasmine replied sarcastically.

Regina yelled at the top of her lungs! "AYE!!!! Now, either y'all can chill out and be civil or y'all can leave. And if you don't leave Ima call the police, and their station is right up the street."

"Well, why don't you tell your lil Afro pick wearing soul sista friend to shut up talking to us then?" DeAndrea retorted.

"Look atcha, just letting all your little ignorant, skanky, hood-ratishness show, BUT what else can we expect from a hood-rat? And I know you can't keep a man." Jasmine impressed sincerely.

"LADIES, FOR THE LAST TIME, CHILL...for me. Now I'm trying to run a professional hair salon. It's not fair that I show y'all love every time y'all come up in here and in return y'all do me like this and possibly make me lose business... Come on y'all we sista's...so let us set aside the drama, and keep the peace." Regina said looking at DeAndrea, and then at Jasmine.

"I'm cool, my bad. I should've never let them get me rattled." Jasmine said as she sat down crossed her legs, and began reading her article again.

Regina looked over at DeAndrea hoping she'll act like she got some since and chill out. DeAndrea just shook her head with a slight nasty look on her face, and eventually sat down. Peace was sort of restored and everything pretty much went back to normal. Damn...sometimes the only way to put all of that work drama behind you is to go home to a peaceful house, take ya clothes off, shower, get a good massage, and some good head

while getting your sip on...and if that's so...I
CAN'T WAIT TO GET THE HELL OFF WORK!!!

CHOICES...LET THEM BE WISE

9:47pm Cognac sat with her legs curled up on her couch watching NBA Housewives. She was snug in her fitted t-shirt and pajama pants. Her show had just gone off so she grabbed her remote and flipped through the channels. Unsatisfied with what was on TV she turned the power off and sat the remote on the coffee table. She slipped her feet into her house shoes, got up, and then picked up her wine glass off the table. She walked into the kitchen and opened up the refrigerator, grabbed the Mascoto and poured her a glass. She took a nice swallow and for some strange reason she had a flash of Marcello. She shook her head and poured a little more wine in her glass. She shut the door and walked up the hallway, and thought about when she first met Keith. She thought about how good of a woman she was to Marcello and how she rejected Keith in the beginning. She walked up the stairwell headed to her room, and clear as yesterday she could hear that ladies sneaky voice asking "You think that's her?" Cognac got to the top of the stair and looked in her room. She took a sip as she looked at her beautiful lonely bed. She walked over and sat her wine down on the night stand. She kicked her house shoes off, grabbed her cell phone out of her Pajama pocket and then flopped on the bed stomach first. She dangled her feet in the air and then dialed Regina.

"Hey, Coney, how you feeling?" Regina asked as she answered the phone.

"I'm feeling pretty good, better." Cognac replied, yawning.

"Good, this little time off and rest is doing you some justice."

"Yeah it is, but what I really need is a serious vacation; you know, have a pocket full of money, pack my bags and catch the next flight to Paris. Do some sightseeing, some shopping, eat some good food, and do some more shopping. You feel me?" Cognac asked in her silly voice.

"Hell yeah, I feel you. Matter of fact we ought to plan that and make it happen."

"I'm with that; all you have to do is let me know when it's the best time for you, and we out." Cognac replied as she rolled over, sitting up in the bed and grabbed her wine.

"OOOHHH Coney, hold up I almost forgot!" Regina said, animated.

"What." Cognac replied very inquisitively.

"Tell me how come ya girl, DeAndrea was about to get her ass whooped up at the salon today." Regina answered.

"What? What happened?" Cognac asked excitedly and sipped her wine.

"You know how she is when she gets to running her damn mouth. She talks to damn much. And today, this chick named Jasmine looked like she was about to put her foot in her ass if we didn't jump in between them before it escalated."

"What?! Her ass is so stupid, I swear. One day she gone catch the right person on the wrong day and they gone beat her ass, and aint nobody gone be there to save her ass either." Cognac said, sipping her drink.

"I know." Regina replied.

"Aye, damn! It was something I was just about to tell you, and it slipped my mind that fast. I hate when I do that." Cognac said.

"I hate when I do that to, and it's always the juicy stuff you be forgetting." Regina replied.

"Oh, I remember. Guess who I saw today." Cognac said.

"Who? Give me a hint." Regina said.

"A old flame of mine who you really wanted me to get with."

"Who? I'm really drawing a blank right now."

"Devin." Cognac answered.

"Devin? I don't remember no Devin?"

"You got to remember Devin, tall, rich brown-skinned, brotha with waves and goatee. I brought him over your house to the party that time." Cognac said as she sipped her drink and sat it down on the nightstand.

"Uuuummmmmm... Oh, yeah I remember him I think. That's that good guy you dissed." Regina said sarcastically.

"Whatever, I was just seeing someone else who interested me more than he did at the time."

"Yeah, Marcello, which wasn't a great idea, duh. Tell me you and Devin hooked back up."

"Girl, first you tell me I don't need to be in a relationship right now, just focus on getting me together and now you telling to get with Devin. Girl, make up your mind." Cognac said sarcastically.

"No, I didn't say make Devin your man, I just think because he's a good man that it would be a good idea if y'all stayed in contact.

Then when you are ready for a man he can be the one you'll consider getting with."

Cognac exhaled and sighed "I mean, he cool, he is a good guy...I just don't know."

"What is it, Coney? Is he's not street enough, he aint thug enough? What is it?"

"C'mon Regina, don't go there." Cognac briefly looked up at the ceiling in frustration because she didn't feel like hearing the truth and then grabbed her wine and took a nice gulp.

"You know why I'm saying this to you, because I was the same way at one point in time. I was attracted to the loud mouth, flashy ballin type dudes that actually wasn't no good for me. And when I had people who truly cared for me telling me to leave them type of dudes alone I didn't want to hear it, and the truth irritated me. I got my lil stank ass attitude and distanced myself from those who were really trying to help me. In the end it was that bad boy I was chasing who hurt me...bottom line I just don't want you being one of them women who choose to date bad boys because that's what you are attracted to and then when you get hurt by him you want to complain that *a good man is hard to find*." Regina expressed sincerely.

"Look, you're right, I know, and Ima be wiser about the type of dudes I choose to date...That's why I told Devin yes when he asked me if he could take me to dinner tomorrow."

"I am so glad for you right now, Coney. I just want you to be happy. I aint telling you to date a nerd or a lame, just a good man that treats you right and has a positive future that benefits you and your son."

"You're right."

"Well, look I know it's getting late and I'm getting sleepy (Yawns) so Ima just holla at you tomorrow."

"Yeah, you sound tired, so just call me when you get up or something."

"Okay...AYE CONEY WAIT, DON'T HANG UP, I GOT A QUESTION. Does that Demarco dude call you and harass you anymore?" Regina asked.

"Naw, I aint heard from him since my birthday. He aint called, he haven't text. I'm sure that man done moved on by now, and trust me I'm so glad." Cognac said as she fiddled with charm on the necklace she was wearing.

"I know, right." Regina said, sounding kind of disheartened.

"Aye, are you okay? You just went from sounding all happy to sounding kind of...down." Cognac asked.

"I know...it's just that mentioning Demarco made me think about Cynthia, and Cedric. Can you really believe it's been eight months? I mean, it feels like it was just yesterday when they were over here in my basement for the Christmas party."

"I know...it's a trip how time flies. I still have a couple of voicemails on my phone that she left me; I don't even want to erase them."

"Oh my God, you too! I swear I still have a couple of voicemails she left me on my phone...I listened to one of them the other day; I cried." Regina said, endearing.

"Yeah...that shit is deep..."

"Aye...will you do me a favor?" Regina asked.

"What's that?"

"Will you please promise me you won't be dating these street thugs and drug dealers no more?"

Cognac took a deep breath and replied "Gina...I promise you I'm done dating them type of dudes...to the best of my ability."

"Coney! Don't play with me."

"Okay, calm down, let me stop playing before you have a baby. Dang, thought you was my Momma for a minute. But for real though, you got my word, I'm done dating them kind of dudes."

"Thank you, boo. Now I can sleep good."

Cognac yawns "Yeah, I'm about to hit the sack too."

"Good, Ima holla at you tomorrow then." Regina said.

"Okay, good night, bay." Cognac said as they hung up.

Cognac swallowed down the rest of her wine and sat the glass down on the nightstand. She folded her pillow just right and snuggled herself in bed and fell asleep. About thirty minutes later she was slightly tossing and turning. Her eyes slightly quivered as she sighed with discomfort. She heard Demarco's voice "WAKE YO ASS THE FUCK UP!!" and the sound of his pistol as he cocked it. Cognac immediately woke up breathing heavily, gasping for air! She realized that she was only dreaming and calmed herself. She turned on her lamp that was on the nightstand. She opened the drawer and pulled out a novel that she had been enjoying. She crossed her legs and lied back reading her book until she fell asleep with the book lying on her chest.

 HAIRWARS

Who are the best hairstylist, men or women?

Today just seemed to be sort of off the hook here in Motown. The Ribs and Soul Festival was the main attraction going on downtown at Hart Plaza. A few big name R&B Artist were performing down there on the underground stage. Adjacent from the underground stage on the other side of the festival was the pyramid stage. They had the Poetry by the River show going on over there hosted by a poet named Men-Tal and another dope poet by the name of Ms. Beloved Aalysis. Downtown Detroit was jumping and everyone was loving the atmosphere. One thang about Detroit folks we love the sunshine. The weekend was forecasted to be an average of eight-seven degrees, sunny with clear skies; and please believe it y'all it's party time. People had been at the mall all day shopping getting fresh to def. And of course...the women here stay fly, and keeping their hair and nails done religiously. So of course, business was booming at Essential Beauty Salon, and everyone was on point. Regina was whipping her client's hair to perfection. She had it cut short and sexy and tapered beautifully in the back. Benita was braiding her client's hair preparing it for a sew-in. On her clients lap lied a Remi Velvet laced front wig with the price tag still on it that read $850.00. Antonio had the women's nails looking absolutely stunning with gorgeous, rich shades, colors and creative designs. And De'Juan was doing what he always does best, arching eyebrows and doing eyelashes. As usual the conversations were spicy and everybody had something to say. Antonio was just about finished with his client, Lakesha's nails. Lakesha was having an interesting conversation with her friend who was sitting next to her.

"For a guy, DeJuan shole know how to lay a sista hair out and hook her eyebrows up beautifully." Lakesha said as she looked over at Tonya.

"Oh yeah, he's the bomb. That's why I'll go to him to get my hair done before I'll go to a woman any day." Tonya replied.

"Why you say that?" Lakesha asked.

"Because I think he's better than most women."

Lakesha sincerely disagreed and replied. "He is good, but I wouldn't go as far as saying he's better than most women because a woman knows a woman's hair better than a man does any day."

"Well, as far as I'm concerned he is." Tonya replied.

"You must like him or do he be hooking your hair up for free?" Lakesha asked being humorously sarcastic.

Tonya subconsciously glanced at Antonio then back at Lakesha "Girl, you was about to make me say something to you, but I can't because Antonio right here." Tonya said, catching herself before she made a comment about De'Juan.

"Don't hold your tongue on the count of me." Antonio said, keeping a steady hand, executing a precision nail design.

"Nall Ima keep that comment to myself, but on some for real shit I just think that he does hair better than most women. Matter of fact Ima be bold and say I think most men will do a woman's better than most women would." Tonya said confidently.

"You really trippin now, but please tell me what makes you say that." Lakesha said, looking at her crazy.

"Damn, this is getting pretty interesting. But keep talking because this is how I learn how women think and feel because I listen and pay attention." Antonio said in a humorous tone of voice but was very serious.

"For one, straight men who do hair are not jealous of how you look nor are they trying to compete with how you look. Therefore they don't have negative feelings and emotions that get in the way of their performance when they're doing your hair. You don't have to worry about them not having you looking top notch and sexy. For instance, look at the top notch job Antonio is doing on your nails right now." Tonya answered.

Antonio glanced at Tonya. "Damn, you got a point."

"Are you serious?" Lakesha asked, sort of surprised at her comment.

"I'm dead serious. Look, it's no secret that women have to many negative feelings and jealousy issues with other. They always want to look better than you, and a lot of times if not most of the time it will cause them to do something to your hair that you might not like." Tonya preached just as Lakesha butted in.

"Okay, hold up, hold up. I feel you on the fact that men love to see a woman look sexy and have no beef with doing a super-fly job on you. However, all women don't have jealously and insecure issues that hinder them from doing a phenomenal job on a woman's hair as well. For one, they take their profession serious and want to be the best at what they do. They understand that when they make a woman's hair look gorgeous other women are going to admire and inquire where she got her hair done at. They know that if they do a good job on you it will ultimately increase business. And trust me she aint gone let no ill feelings come in between her and her money." Lakesha expressed.

"Okay, I feel you, but what about this. Men come into a profession that is predominately ran by women and know that they have to do an extra astounding job in order to stand out and be respected as one of the best. Men are just as competitive as women when it comes down to their work. AND THEN DON'T LET IT BE A GAY MAN because he's really going to try and out-do a woman because inside he wants to be one. They are meticulous perfectionist with everything they do especially when it comes to looks and fashion." Tonya said.

"Ima say this, women are competition specialist, we compete soon as we get up out the bed. And please believe women WILL NOT let men come and outshine them in a profession that they have been notorious in since the beginning of time; I don't give a damn if he's gay, straight, or Zoophilia." Lakesha impressed.

Antonio had to stop and laugh for a moment "Hell nall, what the hell is a Zoophilia?"

"You know, one of them folks that like having sex with animals." Lakesha replied as Tonya busted out laughing, trying not to be too loud.

"Girl, you is ignorant!" Tonya said, laughing.

"Hell nall, that's that bestiality shit. One thing I can say is I know we do some dumb shit, but we don't be doing that type of shit. That is some ole sick, nasty ass shit, and people wonder where a lot of these nasty ass diseases be coming from." Antonio said with a nasty sneer on his face, shaking his head.

Lakesha held her hand up and looked at it when Antonio paused "I must say you have my nails looking out cold especially with this deck of cards design, I'm loving it."

"Thank you Ms. Lady, I appreciate that. Aye, if y'all don't mind I want to add my two cents to y'alls hell of a conversation about who do hair the best." Antonio said.

"Go ahead." Lakesha replied.

"Well, I aint trying to act like I'm a expert when it comes to hair, but I think when it comes down to who does it better, women or men it all depends on the person and how much they understand the science of hair. It also depends on how passionate they are with the art of hair and how much they enjoy doing it. Now I could be wrong but my guess would be that women have a slight advantage because they have dealt with women's hair all of their lives." Antonio expressed as he continued doing her nails.

"I love how diplomatic and intelligent you are, that is so sexy. I wish we could encourage more men to think like you." Lakesha said, finding herself attracted to him that much more.

"RIGHT, I need me a man like that but hell, good men are too hard to find now days." Tonya said, pruning her lips and shaking her head.

"Aye let me share a little something about that good man is hard to find cliché. I aint saying that this applies to y'all two but a lot of women that speak that old cliché are not actually attracted to good men. That's why they keep finding themselves with bad men and in bad relationships because that's what their attracted to. When they meet good men they reject them for some reason or make them a play brother, but never a lover. And the same go for men as well, this don't just apply to women. We all need to stop blaming everybody for the bad choice of people that we choose to date and just be real with it admit our attraction to negativity." Antonio preached.

"So, you mean to tell me that the reason I can't find a good man is because I'm not attracted to them?" Tonya said as she looked at him sideways.

"Hey, I aint trying to say that's what's going on with you, but I am saying that is the case with a lot of people. They aint attracted to humble, nice people; they love drama kings. They think people having attitudes and walking around with mean mugs on their faces is sexy. So if that's what people like then they need to be real with themselves and stop complaining about who aint good out here and just live with their choices." Antonio said, finishing up Lakesha's last nail.

"Well, Ima say this, then pay you and then Ima leave on this note because I gotta be somewhere in the next thirty minutes. But, you are right, a lot of people are attracted to bad boys and bad girls, negativity and attitudes, but on the other hand some people get tricked into bad relationships because they fall for that person's representative. And then down the line after that person has gotten comfortable and feel like you aint going nowhere is when they let their real colors show and that how that type of scenario plays out." Lakesha stated as she fanned her hands for her nails to dry.

"You right, relationships are deep depending on how you see them." Antonio said and excelled.

"See what I'm saying, I aint got no time to be meeting nobodies damn representative because when one of they stupid asses fuck up Ima whoop both they dumb asses! And that's why I'm staying damn single! Sheeeeiiit, Giiiirl bye, I aint the one!" Tonya said very hood, and hilariously with her lips pruned and eyes bucked.

WHAT A MUTHAFUCKIN DAY

An all black 2009 Jeep Liberty pulled up to the valet parking area of the gorgeous historical Renaissance building. The driver's side door opened and a tall brown-skinned brotha stepped out with a well tapered low hair cut, and I nicely sculptured goatee. He wore an off-white, short sleeved designer dress shirt with a fresh architectural Egyptian Pyramid centered in the back with symbols around it. He had on some nice black slacks, and black square-toed dress shoes; Mr. Devin was looking razor sharp. The passenger door opened and Cognac stepped out looking nothing less than stunning. She wore a white designer dress made of soft linen that accentuated her small waist and round hips seductively. She rocked a thick black belt around her waist that complimented her black purse, and five inch black stilettos. Her earrings color coordinated perfectly with what she had on. And just to set off the captivating look she sported the big square-lens sunglasses looking like a straight up movie star. The valet attendant handed Devin a ticket and they headed inside. Her bulgy round ass wiggled like firm cold Jell-O (**The perfect wiggle**) through her dress with every step she took, making people's mouth's salivate. At least three dudes that were sitting in their cars waiting for valet service got checked by their women after getting caught looking hard as hell out the corner of their eyes. Cognac reached for the door to open it but Devin stopped her and opened the door for her.

"My father always taught me to be a gentleman and open the door for a Queen." Devin said with a smile.

"Oh okay, thank you." Cognac replied with a smile as she stepped inside, thinking to herself that he was trying to run bullshit game on her by being such a gentleman.

"You ever been here to eat before?" Devin asked as they headed to the elevator.

"No, but I always heard that this place was nice. I'm loving the scenery." Cognac said as she looked around.

"I love those chandeliers, they look so damn classy." Devin said as they looked up admiring the enormous fixture of bright lights.

Cognac marveled at the prestigious furniture that decorated the floor.

"I promise you you're going to love this place, the food is delicious." Devin said as they stopped at the elevator and he pressed the up button.

"Good because I'm hungry. Ima order some lobster, steak, chicken Alfredo, and some French Fries." Cognac said, playfully.

"Is that it?" Devin asked, being funny as well.

"So what you trying to say?" Cognac asked with an eyebrow raised and her hand on her hip.

"I'm trying to say I hope you're ready to get your grub on." Devin said with a grim, rubbing his hands together.

The elevator doors opened and he held the door open.

"So, you think I'm greedy and fat?" Cognac asked as she stepped on.

Devin laughed and replied. "Not at all. Why you ask that?"

"Just checking." Cognac answered.

Devin looked at her ass as he stepped in behind her and uttered to his self "But that ass is fat and round for sho."

"What was that last part you just uttered, Mr.?" Cognac asked, knowing all along what he said...she just wanted to hear him say it again.

"What you talking about, pretty lady?" Devin asked with a guilty smile on his face, pressing the second floor button.

"Don't pretty lady me, I heard your little remark."

"Well, it is nice. **VERY NICE.**" Devin said.

Cognac just shook her head as they reached the second floor and the doors opened. They stepped out and walked to their right and through the corridors. They looked up at the extremely high ceilings as they walked across the gorgeous catwalk admiring the immaculate ambience. The walkway led to a desk where they were greeted by an attendant.

"Hello, do you two have reservations?" The attendant asked with a smile.

"Yes." Devin answered.

"What's the name?"

"Devin Jamison."

The attendant looked in the reservation book and scrolled down the list with her finger.

"Okay, take the elevator here behind me up to the seventy-first floor. Thank you for coming and enjoy your dinner."

"Thank you." Devin said as he and Cognac went and got on the elevator.

The elevator was beautiful, made out of thick glass allowing a breathtaking overview of the beautiful Detroit River, and Canada. Devin hit the button and they started to rise. They turned around looked out the window at the beautiful scenery of busy life and city lights.

"This is so dope." Devin said as he looked out over the river.

Cognac loved the view as she looked out over everything. She looked over at Devin trying to think what could be wrong with him. He seems to perfect; he got to be running some game on her. All the chivalry from him opening every door, calling her Queen had to be his representative she figured. Her silent defense mechanism kicked in and her smile became a straight face as she looked back out the window. Devin looked over at her and noticed her energy had changed.

"Hey, baby you alright?" Devin asked.

Cognac nodded her head, steady looking out the window "Yeah I'm alright."

"You sure, you kind of just got quiet all of a sudden."

"Yeah, I know, I'm sorry. I just had something on my mind for a second, I'm straight though." Cognac said.

Devin looked at her admirably; he loved the way her dress softly swathed down over her voluptuous figure. He loved her nicely sculpted legs and her dainty, feminine style was a major turn on.

"I swear to God, I love your damn feet. You have the sexiest feet any woman could ever pray for." Devin impressed.

"Boooyy, you know you're good with the words, but thank you. I appreciate the compliment." Cognac said, glancing at her feet then at him.

"Well I promise you I mean it. They are the perfect size with a golden honey brown complexion and your nail design is killing them. Not to mention the way they look in them heels makes me wanna kiss on them." Devin said as he looked up in her eyes.

"So, you got a serious foot fetish going on, huh? What is it about a woman's feet that y'all love so much? I think my feet are okay but I just be curious as of what makes y'all like feet so much." Cognac expressed.

"Well, I can't speak for all brothas but I absolutely appreciate and adore the female anatomy. What makes a woman's feet so appealing to me is the shape, and cleanliness. I love when a woman keeps her nails done; it represents class and good hygiene. If a woman does those things then a man like me with a foot fetish will kiss her feet and suck her toes every damn day and make her feel like she's in paradise." Devin sincerely expressed.

The elevator reached the seventy-first floor and the doors opened to an exquisite restaurant. They stepped out and walked to the desk just ahead of them and gave the service lady his name. The service lady grabbed two dinner menus and led them to their seats just alongside an enormous picture window providing an incredible view. He pulled out her chair for her and she sat down. Damn, it aint like she haven't experienced chivalry before but she couldn't stop thinking that it was part of an ulterior motive. She was cool but silently on guard; patiently awaiting the bullshit to show up just like it always does with the rest of the fellas. The waitress came over and asked them if they were ready to order. They needed a moment to look over the menu to see what they wanted, but they did order a bottle of their best wine, and a couple of waters.

"This place is beautiful; I love the whole set up." Cognac said as she sipped her wine and looked around.

"Yeah, it's very nice. I love this big picture window and how we can look down over the water and Canada. It's gorgeous...just like you." Devin replied and sipped his drink.

"Thank you. This wine is outstanding, it aint bitter, it aint too sweet, it's just right."

"I knew you'd love it, it's a classy place for a classy lady." Devin replied.

"Thank you Devin, you've always been sweet. I'm sure you've got all the ladies all over you as charming and handsome as you are." Looking at his ring finger to see if he had a tan line where a ring would be.

"Nall, I wouldn't say all that; some may say something to me every now and then but not a whole lot." Devin replied, thinking to himself she likes him but she is definitely on guard.

"You must have a girlfriend." Cognac said, paying close attention to his every word.

"Naw, I'm single. I've been single going on a year now."

"Really, what happened? I thought y'all was gone get married the way she had you locked down." Cognac replied.

"She aint have me locked down, it's just that when I'm in a relationship I'm pretty much on chill mode, and with that person."

"So why didn't y'all get married?"

"She became a little to possessive, and wanted every single moment of my time. If I wasn't at work I was with her almost every day and whenever I went out and chilled with the fellas she always had an attitude when I got home."

"Y'all lived together?!" Cognac asked, shocked.

"Nall, we didn't stay together, but it felt like it because we were together basically every day. Bottom line, we didn't make it because of her selfish ways, and her attitudes. And I can't be in a relationship that feels like an imprisonment." Devin stressed as he took another sip of his drink.

"Well, you know us women; we love attention especially from our man."

"And that's fine, but if I want to chill with my family or my friend sometimes I don't want no problems. Why should your family and friends become obsolete because you get in a relationship? That's just straight up selfishness, and I can't stand selfish people."

"She must've been ugly and you always left her at home when it was time to go out with your peeps or something." Cognac said, making a joke.

"Nall it wasn't that. Actually she was a fine ass woman and could have any dude she wanted far as I'm concerned. But her possessive ways is probably why she's a single woman to this day."

"She ever try to get back with you?"

"She do from time to time, but I don't feed into that no more. She's one of them women that play to many emotional mind games, and that shit will always destroy a relationship. Gotta keep it simple. But wait, enough about her and me. What's up with you, are you single?"

"Y e a h, I'm single." Cognac answered and took a nice sip of her wine.

"Wow, you had to take a drink after barely getting that out. You must not be sure of yourself." Devin said, being funny.

"Well, to make a long story short I broke up with a guy last Christmas after I caught him having sex with my ex-girlfriend in my bed. After that I found out that I was pregnant by him, **THEN** found out he was still legally married, or for lack of better words not officially divorced yet. And then he turned around and tried to kill me after I told him I wouldn't get back with him. And then I had met a guy named Keith who I was recently dating and not trying to get to serious with. Recently we started getting a little more serious and we agreed that we would officially be a couple, the night of my birthday. We were at my party and decided to leave out and go to the store and get some more drinks for everybody. And before we even made it to the store we both got shot in his car and he died right then."

Devin looked bewildered and replied "Damn...let's have a toast...to life itself." Devin said as he refilled their glasses full of wine.

One of Cognac's girlfriends, Tamika and her boyfriend had just finished eating and were leaving. Tamika noticed Cognac sitting down having a drink and spoke to her...slightly ghetto-fabulously.

"Coney, wsup girl? I'm glad to see you out and doing better." Tamika said, very excited.

"Thank you T, it feels good to get out and enjoy the day."

"Hey, this is my boyfriend, Claude." Tamika said as Claude shook Cognacs hand.

"And, this is Mr. Devin, a very good friend of mines." Cognac said as Devin shook their hands.

"So, is this your first time coming here since I told you about it?" Tamika asked.

"Yes, and I'm loving it, it's very nice." Cognac answered.

"Hell yeah it's nice, matter of fact this place is the bomb! You hear me?! What they need to do is put a place like this in the hood. They think we won't be spend money up in that mug and get our grub on, but honey trust me business will be fuckin booming, I know! And you know how I know? Because these muthafucka's make some good ass lamb chops, and hood muthafucka's love some fuckin lamb chops!" Tamika said, so hood with her eyes bucked.

Devin just looked at her in disbelief with his mouth slightly opened....

RIBS AND SOUL FEST - HART PLAZA

9:47pm Downtown Detroit was on Jam. The Ribs and Soul was the place to be. Devin and Cognac walked across Jefferson with a group of people at the light. Devin had Cognac stand up under the famous statue of Joe Louis's arm and fist and took her picture with his phone camera. They walked on across the street through clusters of people, many had on neon necklaces and glasses. The delicious smell of Bar-B-Qued food was off the hook making your mouth salivate and ready to eat even if you weren't hungry. They walked over by the underground stage and watched the singing performance that was going on. They stayed there for a while and decided they wanted to go and get something to eat; the food was smelling too good. There were venders everywhere to choose from, and people flocked around looking at the food and standing in lines. Grilled chicken, rich savory bar-b-qued ribs slathered in sauce, shish-kabobs, Philly steak subs etc. They ordered two Philly steak subs and went and sat down and ate. Once they finished eating they walked around admiring the gorgeous art paintings, and enjoying all the music. A young man with a hand full of neon necklaces walked up to them.

"Hello, would you like to buy some of my necklaces tonight?" The young man asked.

"Yeah, let me get two of them." Devin said as he reached in his pocket, pulled out some money and paid him.

The young man gave him the necklaces and left. Devin took one of the necklaces and placed it around Cognac's neck. Cognac smiled and replied "Thank you."

"You welcome, sweetie." Devin said, seeming to have a hard time fastening the necklace around his neck.

Cognac politely took the necklace from him and fastened it around his neck.

"I am really enjoying myself today, this is so fun." Cognac said, smiling.

"I'm glad you're enjoying yourself babe, I'm enjoying myself to. I appreciate you coming out with me."

"My pleasure." Cognac replied, finding herself liking him.

"Let's go over here to the pyramid stage where they got the Poetry by the River show going on." Devin said.

"I'm following you." Cognac replied.

Devin gently took her by the hand and led her over to the other show. His hand felt so good and masculine holding hers. She thought to herself she should've gotten with him instead of Marcello and she would've never went through any of this drama. There were two poets hosting the show going by the names of Men-Tal, and Aalysis. There was a band on stage by the name Soul Planet sounding fantastic and they played behind the well known Detroit vocalist Ms. Katrina Storm. The performance was incredible and everyone was loving it. Damn it feels good to be in Detroit right now!!

A NIGHT TO REMEMBER

12:37pm. Devin pulled up in front of a house, just across the street from Cognac's house. They were feeling great after a complete day full of fun, good eats, and entertainment. They sat in the car talking for a little moment before she went in. He had on the perfect music and the moon was shinning down on them beautifully through the moon-roof.

"I feel so good right now, thank you again for such a beautiful day." Cognac said sincerely.

"Aw, baby you're welcome, I enjoyed myself to. Hopefully this won't be the last time." Devin said as he softly touched her hand.

"Yeah, we can do that, just let me know when."

"I promise you I will."

"You know they got a play that's going to be down at the Fox Theatre in three weeks." Cognac said, hinting.

"Oh yeah, what play?"

"Why Do Good Girl's Like Bad Boys?" Cognac answered.

Devin briefly looked away out of the window showing a slight bit of disgust and replied. "Awwww damn, another one of them stereo typing, male bashing plays."

"What you talking about, why you call it that?" Cognac asked.

"Because it is, just look at the title. Why Do Good Girls Like Bad Boys? Automatically you think about a good little innocent woman being taken advantage of and done wrong by some no good man. You don't ever hear about plays titled Why Do Good Men Like Bad Women? It's often very sexist and unfairly portrays a negative image on us men. Then the women go and watch these plays and get all emotional about it and start unfairly judging men and teaching their children how men are bad without giving them a balanced outlook on relationships." Devin spoke profoundly.

"Baby, I think you looking at it to deep."

"Naw sexy girl, you just aint looking at it deep enough. I aint saying that men aint out here doing dumb shit, but just don't half way tell the story because women are out here doing the same dumb stuff as well. Or come up with a title that aint unbalanced like Why Do Good Folks Like Bad Folks or something like that."

"I mean, I understand what you're saying, it can appear one sided. We aint gotta go to that one, its other plays we can see."

"Don't get me wrong we can go see it, I just get tired of these producers pimping that overridden, male bashing storyline."

As they talked they never saw the dark figure that was slowly coming forward from in between the houses just behind Cognac. Moonlight slightly glared upon Demarco's face as he stood there in the dark. The pistol in his hand gleamed as he slowly eased forward. His heart thumped heavy with anger and hate as he looked at Cognac and Devin hugging each other. His nostrils flared, and his jaw tightened as he breathed harder. Devin and Cognac looked at this weird looking dude that was walking up the street looking in between the houses. They never noticed Demarco at all. Cognac kept her eye on him as she opened the door and got out of the car. Demarco swiftly walked up on her!

"So that's how the fuck it's laying!!" Demarco asked, enraged with a mean ass scowl on his face.

Cognac turned around and could do nothing but stand there with a face full of terror as her heart beat rushed.

The strange man that was walking up the street looking in between the houses quickly pulled out a pistol and aimed it at Demarco before he could do anything. The strange man yelled "Put the gun down, Demarco, and don't move!"

Everything happened so damn fast, Devin couldn't do shit but be shocked by all the random happenings. Demarco was surprised and caught off guard as multiple police cars whipped up on the scene. More police officers immediately got out of their cars with their weapons drawn. The strange man that was walking up the street was an undercover officer who was trailing Demarco. Demarco couldn't believe he had been followed.

"Demarco, put the gun down, and slowly back away from it!" The officer yelled again.

Demarco took a deep breath and looked at Cognac with eyes bleeding with hate. He knew that he had to comply with the officers and surrender peacefully or resist arrest and die violently. The look on his face became nastier as his eyes slightly squinted, griming

Cognac ominously. His grip tightened on the pistol and his index finger was locked around the trigger. He glanced at the officers, and then slowly eased down. Quickly blasting her then turning around and running shot through his mind for a split second. He calmly placed the gun on the ground and rose up interlocking his fingers behind his head. Police officers rushed him and immediate cuffed him while reading him his rights. Demarco just stared at Cognac as they walked him over to the squad car and put him inside the back seat. A couple officers spoke with Cognac and Devin trying to get whatever information they could. Demarco stared out the back window at Cognac as the officers rode off into the night.

LUAU TIME

It is said that after every storm the sunshine has to cut its way through and make you forget that it was ever there. No need to let all the past drama keep you feeling down for ever. It actually gives you a reason to celebrate life and a new progression. It's a week later after all the perplexing violence...
9:51pm Regina's party was live as hell, and everybody and their momma was over there. From the front of the house you could hear the music and festivities going on in the back making everyone in the vicinity want to come party. A trail of Malibu track lights aligned a path of octagon shaped patio paved blocks for people to step on led to the backyard. Two TiKi bamboo torches burned as you entered the backyard. Multi-colored TiKi garden lights hung just above creating the perfect lighting effect for the occasion. "Step in the Name of Love" by R-Kelly, played and serenaded the soul as people stepped in unison on the wood-grained dance floor. The theme was compromised as many wore Lei Garlands around their necks and straw hats

on their heads. Off to the left Chef Chris put on a hell of a show as fire raised from the pan as he cooked. The entrée was sautéed fresh Tilapia fish topped with chopped mango fruit in a light mango salsa with lemon zest and minced parsley sprinkled on top. Simply put, this event made everyone agree on one thing, even if they never agreed on anything else...this was the best damn Luau they had ever been to. "Six no!" someone yelled out as Benita walked past the Bid Whist table. She walked up on the deck and into Regina's house. Benita shut the sliding patio door behind her and walked over to Regina who was briefly looking down reading a magazine.

"Girl, this party is the bomb, and that fish that chef is out there cooking is off the chain!" Benita said as she took a sip of her strawberry daiquiri through her circular party straw.

"I know babe, I'm so glad you came through and helped me get things set up." Regina replied as she took a swallow of her margarita.

"And it's some fine looking fellas out there to! Hell, I feel like I'm at a damn candy store." Benita said with emphasis as she glimpsed outside.

"I know, especially Lawrence friend he brought with him." Regina said.

"Who, where he at?" Benita asked, hilariously and animated.

"Over there playing Bid Whist in that red shirt, and red hat."

"That sundress you got on is ridiculous sexy! I love the whole tropical color scheme you got going along with that Aloha theme. Ya know what I mean?" Benita said, hilariously.

Regina laughed and replied "It's not an Aloha; it's a Luau, silly."

"Well, it can be Hawaii day for all I care, but for now I'm digging that dress. Where you get it from?" Benita asked, touching the fabric.

"From Simply Sexy, right up there on Livernoise."

"I keep saying Ima go up there. Next time I come over here in the day time or just one day when I got some free time Ima stop up there." Benita said as she leaned back up against Regina's island stove in the middle of the kitchen.

Cognac and Devin walked up on the deck and came in the house with Garland around their necks and daiquiris in their hands.

"Wsup y'all!" Cognac asked as she gave Regina and Benita a hug.

"I'm so glad y'all made it." Regina said, joyfully.

"Do I ever miss any of the Luau's or gatherings we have? Plus, after all this hard work you had me doing, helping put this thing together, girl bye, I'm spending the night." Cognac said jokingly.

"Um, you miss a lot of shit, but we aint gone speak on that right now." Regina replied sarcastically.

"Girl, whatever; Anyhow, let me introduce y'all to Devin. Well, Regina you already met Devin, I think, but Benita this is Devin, and Devin this is Benita, and I think you remember Regina." Cognac said, introducing them.

"Yeah, I remember Regina." Devin said as he politely hugged them both.

They chilled in the kitchen for a while talking, laughing, and having drinks, just enjoying the night. The vibe was incredible and people were out there gigging on the dance floor. Peaches wanted another margarita so she took Antonio by the hand and led him off of the dance floor and into the house with everybody else.

"I need another margarita with the quickness!" Peaches said, feeling good.

"Hell yeah, me to." Antonio concurred.

Cognac and Peaches hugged each other and introduced Antonio and Devin. Regina made up another big pitcher of margarita, and poured everybody some.

"Hey, Peaches I see you and Antonio out there on the dance floor showing off." Regina said.

"Nall boo, what you saw was me out there on the dance floor putting it down on him." Peaches said nonchalantly as she glanced at him then back at Regina.

"Regina, I don't know what you slipped in her margarita that got her talking crazy, but if anything I put it down on her. I had her calling me daddy like she always do when I'm putting it down." Antonio said as he popped his collar and sipped his drink.

"Boy, you couldn't handle all this on my bad day! That's if I ever had a bad day! But um...with me you never have a dull moment anyway." Peaches said as she put her hands on her waist and looked down at her hips and ass.

"Aye, I think all of us women need to go out here on this dance floor and put it down on these men." Benita suggested as she downed her drink.

"I agree, let's do it if they aint scared." Peaches added.

"Scared? Girl, we aint never scared. Let's go." Antonio said, hyped.

They all headed outside to hit the dance floor. Regina told them to go ahead and she'll be out there in a moment. Regina had Cognac hold on while everyone else left out. She leaned back up against her counter with her drink.

"Wsup, boo?" Cognac asked, as she walked over sipping her drink.

"Aye, remember that guy Marlon from your birthday party?" Regina asked.

"Yeah, I remember him. What's going on with him?"

"Nothing too much, but let me ask you. Are you and him kicking it on the low or something? I was a little confused with that whole situation that night."

"Oh nall, I aint kicking it with him on no level, and aint trying to either."

"You think something's wrong with him?"

"Nall, I'm not saying that. I'm just saying that right now in my life, I'm trying to chill and take it easy. I'm not looking for a man at the time, but I am enjoying my connection with Devin, other than that I aint thinking about dating nobody else."

"Right, I feel you on that note." Regina said, nodding her head.

"But wsup though? Looks like somebody trying to step out of their own busy box and finally date for a change." Cognac said, smiling."

"Aw, it aint like I don't date...I've just been...busy."

"Gina, when the last time you've been on a date, tell me?" Cognac asked.

"Ummm."

"See what I mean? You can't even remember when the last time was."

"It aint like it's been that long ago, I mean like five of six months maybe."

"Girl, do you like Marlon?" Cognac asked.

"I aint saying all that. Reonna told me a couple days ago that he had asked about me and he wanted me to call him." Regina said, sipping her drink.

"Okay...call him." Cognac said while looking at her like what is she waiting on.

"I guess I will."

"Why don't you call him now and see if he wants to come over tonight and chill with us."

"I'm not about to disturb that man. He's probably tired from work."

"Girl, if that man has been inquiring about you, trust me he won't give a damn about you calling him right now. I bet you he'll be more than happy for you to call him."

"You think so, huh?" Regina asked, bashful.

"Yes, I know so. Now I know you are the big cuz, and you always giving me good guidance, but trust little cuz on this time. Now I'm about to go out here with everybody and you go and call Marlon. And don't come out here without him next to you." Cognac said as she refilled her margarita cup and walked out.

Regina walked into her living room with her margarita and sat down on her couch. She took a sip and scrolled through her text messages because Reonna had texted her Marlon's number. She called him and like Cognac said he answered and was happy that she had called. After a good brief conversation Regina invited him over and he came through. Regina was happy when he called her and told her that he was outside. They kicked it for a while before they walked in the backyard and chilled with everybody else. **2:30am** rolled around and everyone had left except for Cognac, Devin, Marlon, Peaches, Antonio and Benita. They sat in a circle of chairs enjoying the last bit of great conversation and drinks. Regina was feeling super great and stood up.

"I just want to thank every last one of y'all for making this night a beautiful experience, and one to remember. Right now I want to propose a toast...to the rest of this year being beautiful and prosperous for us all. For having the best salon in the business, to true and sincere friends that are hard to find, to Cynthia, may God bless her to have a safe and full recovery, and to Cedric, may he rest in peace. And to us having one of the classiest, livest Luau's ever." Regina said as they all kissed their glasses together at the same time for one hell of a toast.

Now that's how you have a Luau...Salon Talk style...Peace and hair grease y'all.

A Moment of Clarity

The moment the gun went off and Cynthia was shot she fell to the floor. In the process of falling she knocked her head against the edge of the nightstand. The impact caused bleeding on the brain which resulted in her slipping into a coma for all that time. Unfortunately she also contracted what is known as septicemia from the bullet that entered her body. Septicemia is a poisonous and deadly infection in the blood and has to be treated immediately. Like many cases her infection was reoccurring and eventually it caused her demise two months later, October 2011. Cynthia and Cedric were two loving people caught in an uncalled for circumstance that never had to happen. Often we rather harbor anger and react heartlessly before we use peaceful resolutions to resolve our problems. Where there is no peace there is war. Where there is war...there is violence.

RIP

Also by Men-Tal

Salon Talk 3 – KISMET

"Sneak Peek"

THE MOMENT OF REDEMPTION

Downtown Detroit, 3:10am a truck pulled into a very dark alleyway just in between two buildings. The headlights get turned off as the truck quietly pulled to the side and parked. Her large black Panama Swinger Hat veiled her face, hiding her eyes as she looked around the parameter vigilantly. The building to the left was vacant with a large filthy garbage dumpster up against it. The building on the right had three businesses connected to each other, a beauty shop, a shoe store and a bar. All the lights were out because the businesses were closed. She turned the engine off and then reached over and opened up the glove box. With black gloves on she pulled out a black automatic pistol, a fully loaded clip and then shut the glove box. She looked at her watch, and it read 3:12am. She slid the clip in, cocked the pistol and got out the truck shutting the door behind her. She wore a long black dress, full length black trench coat and black high heel boots which allowed her to blend perfectly with the night. She looked around and made sure the coast was clear and no one was watching. She walked forward and peeked around the back of the building to her right. No one was in sight so she proceeded. The heels of her boots lightly click clacked across the wet concrete as she carefully walked towards the back door. Her coat and dress slightly flared in the wind behind her. The streetlights were all out in the immediate area providing the perfect camouflage. The faint glare of moonlight barely spilled through the sides of the buildings hardly providing any visibility. A stack of very old wooden doors with chipped paint peeling off were leaning up against the back of the building. She heard a strange sound then it suddenly stopped... Could it be someone waiting in the shadows ready to put a bullet through her heart? She paused in her tracks and looked around ready and willing to commit homicide. She didn't see anything and then she cautiously moved forward. SUDDENLY OUT OF NOWHERE SOMETHING CAME RUNNING OUT FROM BEHIND THE RAGGEDY DOORS!! SHE IMMEDIATELY AIMED HER GUN; READY TO BLAST... till she realized that it was just a cat running off with a small rat in its mouth. She took a deep breath and calmed herself as she looked at her watch again; it read 3:14am. She knew the moment of redemption was so close that she could taste it on her tongue. Everything was pretty much quiet as a ghost town. You could hear the faint sound of traffic riding by over on Woodward Street, and a couple of wind chimes hanging from above. QUICKLY SHE LOOKED AS THE DOOR UNLOCK!! Her heartbeat thumped a little harder, and her breathing accelerated as her eyes dilated. She gripped the pistol with both hands tightly. With a face full of anger and hate she got her stance and planted her feet firmly. She heard the turning of the door knob!! THE DOOR OPENED AND!!!!.................

SALON TALK 3- KISMET Coming this February 2012

Other Books By Men-Tal

Salon Talk: A Topic of Discussion

A Lil Cognac Ta Get Ya Mind Right Alright, for the time being I'm the Topic of Discussion. Who am I you ask? I'm Rachelle, but my friends call me Cognac or Coney for short because whenever we're having a discussion or I have an opinion about something I give it to you straight with no ice, and no cola. So if you can't handle the truth then I suggest that you keep your mouth shut and your thoughts to yourself. However, I'm sort of messed up in the head right now because I'm sitting here in my GORGEOUS kitchen staring at the glass from my BEAUTIFUL kitchen table shattered all over the floor and a trail of blood leading out the front door. Now I'm sure you would like to know what the hell is going on here, but look...I need yall to give me a moment to clean this mess up, take me a good hot bath, and get dressed. Its ladies night over at Lacey's Bar and Grill so just meet me over there and I'll explain to you what just happened... Blood is too hard to get off the floor if you leave it on there for too long...Damn I need a drink. Sincerely Cognac

SPIT

As if the pain was not enough...witnessing the murder of his childhood peers and having his best friend, Diangelo take his last breath in his arms...As if the deception, controversy, relationship issues, nightlife and violence is not enough to make a good man loose his sanity and religion... sometimes the micro-phone and spotlight is a man's sanctuary and redemption

...Life...is like a loaded gun pointed at your head leaving you with two options live or die and one question...What would you do?

Silent Screams

online book sites

Silent Screams is a collection of thought provoking poems that elaborate on the many aspects of our lives ranging from love, relationships, intimacy, and much more.

Salon Talk: A Topic of Discussion, SPIT and Silent Screams are available for purchase on your major

Contact Information Page

Men-Tal
Novelist/ Poet/ Art Illustrator
CEO of Essential Expressions
Wordsmith for personalized cards
For Birthdays, Holidays Greetings,
Weddings
Baby Showers, Just because, Condolence
etc.
Illustrator of the art pieces "Delicious as Sin
and Procedure of a 187"
WritingExtraordinaire@yahoo.com

Gentle Touch Phlebotomy Education, LLC
Chantelle R. White CEO/ Director/
Instructor
23300 Greenfield RD Suite 212
Oak Park MI, 48237
Gentletouch.org
> "Where drawing blood is more than a
> skill it's an art"
> "We're changing lives one blood draw at
> a time"

<u>AIM- All In Mind Designs</u>
Maurice Ingram
Graphics Designer/ Art Illustrator
Illustrator of the art piece "Love Broken"
Hanufel8@yahoo.com

<u>D&E Photography</u>
Darius Blackmon
Photographer
(313)-734-2005
<u>Grand Diva's Hair and Nail Salon</u>
Cocoa
Hair Stylist
(313)350-4024
Grand.diva@comcast.net